CYRA

Cyra

For information contact :
(authorbanapsha@gmail.com)
https://www.authorbanapsha.com/contact

Book and Cover design by Banapsha

ISBN: 978-93-344-1687-9
First Edition: September, 2025

10 9 8 7 6 5 4 3 2 1

CYRA

CHAPTER 1

Coffee, Blood, and Pen Scratches

Chandigarh doesn't smell like crime.

It smells like wet leaves crushed under hurried footsteps, petrol fumes curling from rickshaws, and overpriced coffee from Sector 17 cafés where influencers pose beside latte art like it's holy scripture. But tonight, standing outside a shuttered furniture shop in Sector 22, with police vans parked like drunk elephants and yellow tape flapping like a tattered flag in the monsoon wind, I could smell it.

Copper. Sharp. Metallic.

Blood.

I cradled my paper cup of double espresso like it was life support, the heat seeping into my fingers, anchoring me. My pen tapped against my notebook in a rhythm only I understood; staccato, erratic, like a heartbeat trying to outrun a nightmare.

Some cops chew gum. Some smoke. Me? I write and drink coffee until my pulse could outpace a train.

"Cyra, victim identified," a constable called out, voice cracking like a teenager's. Rookie. His eyes darted toward the body, then away, like it might reach out and grab him.

I crouched beside the corpse. Male. Mid-40s. White shirt soaked scarlet, clinging to his chest like a lover unwilling to let go. A businessman, if his gold watch wasn't lying. His face was almost serene; except for the way his jaw had been slit and peeled back with surgical precision. The skin flayed open like a grotesque smile, revealing teeth and sinew in a parody of joy.

Arranged. Not just killed. Displayed.

The killer's crimes were their art.

Blood had pooled beneath him, thick and glistening, reflecting the flickering neon from a nearby sign advertising "Discount Sofas." It looked like a portal to somewhere darker. The rain hadn't washed it away. It had only thinned it, smeared it into abstract shapes across the pavement. A Rorschach test for the damned.

I should've felt horror. Instead, I found myself studying the angles, the staging. Like an audience at an exhibition no one was meant to see. The body was posed; arms outstretched, palms open, fingers slightly curled. Like he was offering himself to God. Or daring Him to intervene.

"Cyra."

The gravelly voice pulled me back.

Sebastian stood a few feet away, rain dripping off his ancient leather jacket like tears from a forgotten statue. Retired ACP. Father figure. Pain in my ass. His eyes were tired, the kind of tired that sleep couldn't fix. The kind that came from seeing too many things that shouldn't exist.

"You've been staring at corpses too long," he said.

"Better company than most people in this city." I took a sip. Burnt my tongue. Worth it.

He sighed, the sound heavy with history. "Victim's name is Mahesh Khurana. Import-export business. Notorious for bribery cases. Walked free every time."

"So our killer's got a moral streak," I said, scribbling. Pen scratching fast, faster, like it wanted to outrun my brain. "An artist and a preacher. Chandigarh's own Picasso with a knife."

Sebastian gave me that look. Half pity, half warning. "Don't romanticize it."

"Too late," I muttered.

Behind us, Sector 22's neon lights flickered in the drizzle like dying stars. A few reporters were already circling like vultures, shoving mics toward the barricades. DSP Sharma barked at constables to push them back. Standard.

I turned back to the body. The slit jaw. The offering hands. The message screamed through every detail.

And I understood it better than I should have.

The killer hadn't just murdered Mahesh. They'd sculpted him. The incision was clean, deliberate. Not a rage kill. Not a panic. This was ritual. The jaw had been pulled back and pinned with thin metal rods; surgical, almost dental. I leaned closer. The rods were etched. Tiny symbols. Sanskrit? No. Something older. Something wrong.

"Cyra, you need to see this," a forensic tech whispered, holding out a blood-smeared envelope. It had been tucked beneath the body, like a love letter to the abyss.

I opened it with gloved fingers. Inside was a single sheet of paper, thick and textured, like handmade parchment. Written in crimson ink; no, not ink. Blood.

"He spoke lies with a golden tongue. I gave him truth."

I felt the words crawl across my skin. Not just a message. A manifesto.

Sebastian read over my shoulder, his breath fogging in the cold. "This isn't just a murder. It's a sermon."

I nodded. "And we're the congregation."

The rain intensified, drumming against the pavement like war drums. The city around us kept moving; cars honking, people laughing in distant cafés; but here, in this alley of shadows and blood, time had stopped.

"Cyra," a constable called out again, voice tighter now. "There's something else."

He led us behind the shop, where the dumpster sat bloated with refuse. The lid was ajar.

Inside, nestled among broken furniture and rotting cardboard, was a second body.

Smaller. Younger.

Female.

Her eyes were open, glassy, staring at the sky like it had betrayed her. Her mouth was sewn shut with black thread, lips puckered unnaturally. Her hands were bound with silk ribbon, tied in a bow. A gift.

I swallowed hard. "This wasn't in the report."

"Wasn't found until now," the constable said. "We thought it was just trash."

Sebastian cursed under his breath. "Two victims. Different styles. Same killer?"

I crouched again, pen trembling slightly. The girl's skin was pale, almost blue. No blood around her. No violence, at least not visible. But the stitching… it was meticulous. Each knot perfect. Each loop identical. Whoever did this had patience. And obsession.

"She's not posed like the man," I said. "She's hidden. Like a secret."

Sebastian nodded. "Or a confession."

I scribbled faster. The espresso had kicked in, my thoughts racing. The killer was telling a story. Mahesh was the lie. The girl was the truth. One displayed. One discarded. A dichotomy. A philosophy.

I stood, rain soaking through my coat. "We need to find out who she is. And we need to find out what Mahesh was hiding."

Sebastian looked at me, eyes dark. "You think this is just the beginning?"

I didn't answer. I didn't need to.

Because somewhere in the city, someone was already preparing their next canvas.

And I was already listening for the pen scratches in the dark.

CHAPTER 2

Coffee, Clues, and Fingerprints

The CFSL Chandigarh building smelled like antiseptic, ink, and someone else's obsession.

Perfect.

The scent clung to the walls like old secrets. Bleach masked the blood, but not the madness. I walked in, notebook clutched in one hand, coffee in the other, steam curling like smoke from a gun barrel. The fluorescent lights buzzed overhead, casting everything in a sterile glow that made even the living look embalmed.

"Cyra Singh," I said to no one in particular, though everyone here already knew my name. Twenty-eight. Sub-Inspector. Too young for the reputation I carried, too old for the innocence I'd buried. Some cops whispered about my methods.

Criminals whispered worse. I liked that. Fear was a tool. Admiration was a distraction.

"Morning, Ma'am," a lab assistant mumbled, eyes glued to the body photos I'd emailed ahead. His fingers trembled slightly as he adjusted the screen. I watched him, watched the way his gaze flicked from image to image like he was afraid they'd blink.

The first thing I noticed: the hands.

Mahesh Khurana's hands were almost manicured. Polished. The nails gleamed under the lab lights, unnaturally clean. The fingerprints were pristine. Not smudged. Not erased. Preserved. Whoever had touched him had done so with surgical intent; trying to erase evidence without erasing the performance.

I sipped my coffee. Bitter. Burnt. Just how I liked it. My pen tapped against the notebook, a rhythm that matched the hum of the machines. Tapping. Thinking. I was good at this. Too good.

"Cyra, your notes?" Sebastian's voice cut through the static.

He leaned against the doorway, rain still dripping from his jacket like the ghosts he carried. His eyes scanned the room, then settled on me. He was the only person who ever looked at me and saw the edges I hid. The jagged ones.

"Already scanned," I said, flipping the notebook open. "Three distinct knife angles. Perfect symmetry in the chest display. Whoever did this knows anatomy and art." I sketched quickly in the margin; a rough outline of the wounds, the geometry of violence. "Maybe even trained in sculpture or painting."

Sebastian frowned. “Or someone who reads too many crime magazines.”

I smirked. “Don’t insult Picasso, old man. He wouldn’t like it.”

The lab assistant pointed at the screen. “We found partial fingerprints on the desk near the crime scene. Not the usual smudges. Very clean. Almost… intentional.”

I leaned in. The prints were faint, but distinct. A swirl of ridges, a whisper of identity. Not enough for a match. Just enough to tease.

“A copycat?” I asked aloud, almost casually. But inside, my mind twitched. Copycat. A nice scapegoat. Easy narrative for the media. A distraction. A decoy.

Sebastian’s eyes narrowed. “Don’t get ahead of yourself.”

I scribbled more notes, careful to include the right clues for the story I wanted the world to see. A little twist here. An exaggerated deduction there. By the time the media caught wind, they’d already buy the “Copycat theory.” Perfectly innocent; except it wasn’t.

We drove to PGI Chandigarh for the post-mortem. A two-minute ride through neon-lit streets, the rain turning reflections into swirling blood puddles. The city looked like it was bleeding.

Inside the post-mortem room, the air was colder. Sharper. The walls were tiled in white, but the stains never truly left. Dr. Mehra, the forensic pathologist, stood beside the slab, gloves slick with antiseptic and truth.

“Precision cuts,” she said, her voice clinical. “No defensive wounds. He was conscious during the first incision. This was done deliberately. Over time. The killer had patience. A twisted patience."

I nodded, scribbling. Twisted. Patience. Killer. These words mattered. They shaped the narrative. They made the crime art.

Sebastian whispered, almost to himself, "You've seen this before, haven't you?"

I laughed lightly. "Seen? Studied. Every case teaches you something. The question is, do you listen?"

He shook his head. "Be careful, Cyra. The deeper you go, the more dangerous it gets."

I smiled, tapping my pen again. Dangerous was my middle name.

Dr. Mehra peeled back the sheet, revealing the chest cavity. The cuts were symmetrical, almost beautiful. The sternum had been split cleanly, ribs spread like wings. No jagged edges. No hesitation. The heart had been left intact, untouched. A statement.

"The killer wanted us to see this," I said. "Not just the death. The design."

Dr. Mehra nodded. "It's surgical. But also… theatrical."

I leaned closer. The skin had been peeled back in layers, each fold precise. Like a dissection. Or a performance. The blood had dried in thin lines, like brushstrokes. The killer hadn't just killed Mahesh. They'd painted him.

Sebastian's jaw tightened. "This isn't just murder. It's ritual."

I flipped to a fresh page in my notebook. "We need to find out what Mahesh was hiding. And who knew enough to expose it like this."

Outside, the media frenzy had grown. Reporters shouted, flashes of cameras lit up the rain, microphones shoved through barricades like weapons. My copycat narrative had already taken hold. I smiled politely, letting the world chase the wrong story while I traced the real lines of the killer's art.

Because this wasn't random.

This was curated.

And I already knew; better than anyone else; what the canvas would look like next.

CHAPTER 3

Rain, Shadows, and the Canvas to Come

The rain hadn't stopped.

It fell in sheets, relentless and cold, turning Chandigarh's streets into slick veins of light and reflection. Sector 17's neon signs shimmered in puddles like fractured mirrors, each ripple distorting reality just enough to make you question what was real. The city looked like it was bleeding light.

I walked with Sebastian beside me, notebook in hand, pen tapping an erratic rhythm against my thigh. Every step felt like a punctuation mark in a story only I could tell. A story that wasn't finished. A story that might never be.

"Cyra, calm down," Sebastian muttered, pulling his collar higher against the drizzle. His voice was low, gravel dragged across wet stone. "You're bouncing off the walls again."

I shrugged. "Coffee, sleep deprivation, adrenaline. Nothing new."

He didn't laugh. He rarely did anymore.

Our first stop was Mahesh Khurana's apartment in Sector 26. A high-rise with glass balconies and fake potted plants. The kind of place that tried to look expensive but smelled like mildew and regret. The elevator creaked as it rose, the kind of sound that made you wonder if it was carrying ghosts.

We were here for witnesses. Neighbors. Staff. People who saw or heard something before the police arrived. People who didn't know they were already part of the narrative.

The maid was first. Trembling, eyes wide, voice cracking like old porcelain. She clutched the edge of her dupatta like it was a lifeline.

"Sir… he… he didn't come home last night," she stammered. "I… I heard noises… like… arguing. Strange man outside… tall… hooded."

I scribbled rapidly, careful to write her words but emphasize the unknown "stranger" as an open-ended clue. Perfect. A witness clue that could mean anything… including nothing. A shadow in the fog. A ghost in the frame.

Sebastian frowned. "You're pushing too hard. Let her speak."

I leaned back, smiling faintly. "Relax, old man. I'm listening. Just… thinking."

The building's security footage was grainy, black-and-white, like a horror film from the '70s. It showed a shadowy figure leaving at midnight. The face wasn't clear, but the posture; careful, deliberate, almost theatrical; gave me chills. And a thrill.

"Notice the hands," I whispered to Sebastian. "Clenched just so. Balanced. Whoever this is… considers murder a craft."

He gave me a look, half awe, half fear. "Cyra, you're romanticizing this too much."

Maybe. But there's a difference between romance and recognition. Some killers leave sloppy trails. Some… craft a signature. I've always admired the signature ones. Not for what they do. But for how they do it. The precision. The message. The art.

We moved on to the next witness. The accountant. A man in his 50s, twitchy and sweating despite the AC. His shirt clung to him like guilt.

"He… he had enemies," he said, voice barely above a whisper. "Many. Court cases. People threatened him. But I… I don't know… he kept records, receipts… everything in order."

I nodded, pen scratching fast. Organized, like a gallery catalogue. Every victim's life; or death; was being curated. The killer wasn't just choosing targets. They were choosing exhibits.

Sebastian stayed silent, studying me as much as the witnesses. I noticed. Always noticed. "You're quiet. Thinking I'm spiraling?" I teased.

He didn't answer. Good. Let him wonder.

We returned to the crime branch office in Sector 26 Police Lines. The rain followed us, tapping against the windows like impatient fingers. Inside, the air smelled like damp paper and old coffee. My desk was cluttered with maps, timelines, photos. Red string connected dots that didn't want to be connected. And at the center of it all: the "unknown figure."

I'd highlighted them repeatedly. In witness statements. In footage. In my own notes. The copycat narrative was already seeded. Every hint, every lead, every discrepancy; all pointing outward. Not inward. A phantom for the public to chase. A distraction. A decoy.

I sat at my desk, pen hovering over paper, the ink trembling like it knew what I was about to write.

Sebastian finally spoke. His voice was low. Measured. "Cyra… something about this isn't right. I can feel it."

I smiled, tapping my pen again. "Old man, paranoia suits you. But relax; we'll catch this guy. Or girl. Or whatever walks in the shadows."

But inside, a part of me whispered; that I already knew who would be the next canvas. That the "unknown figure" everyone feared… wasn't unknown at all.

Because art, after all, is best appreciated before the truth ruins the illusion.

And this killer? They weren't just painting with blood.

They were painting with memory.

CHAPTER 4
Shadows on the Front Page

By morning, Chandigarh's newspapers had a new headline:

"The Sculptor Strikes Again? Copycat Killer in Sector 22?"

Even the online portals lit up with speculation. Crime blogs, local news apps, and anonymous forums buzzed like hornets. The city was awake, caffeinated, and panicking. I sipped my own coffee, pen in hand, and read the reports with detached amusement. Perfect. My carefully planted threads were already being spun by journalists who had no idea they were dancing to my tune.

The media was predictable. Feed them a whisper, and they'd scream it into a storm.

Sebastian leaned against my desk, arms crossed, his silhouette framed by the grey morning light filtering through the blinds. His eyes were tired, but sharp. "You did this."

I lookcd up, eyebrows raised. "Did what?"

"Shaped the narrative. Made the copycat seem real. You've been feeding the press."

I smirked, swirling the last sip of espresso in my cup. "I'm feeding the truth… selectively. There's a difference."

He didn't smile. "You're playing with fire."

"Fire's the only thing that burns clean."

The desk phone rang. A shrill interruption. I picked it up, pen still tapping against my notebook.

DSP Sharma's voice came through, clipped and official: "Cyra, we have a lead on the supposed copycat. The man's name is Rajiv Malhotra. Journalist. Failed career. Obsessed with crime stories. Lives alone in Sector 37."

I tapped my pen harder. Rajiv. Perfect profile. Fringe journalist with just enough access to crime scenes to be a suspect. The kind of man who'd linger near barricades, ask too many questions, write too few articles. A voyeur with a keyboard.

Sebastian growled. "We can't arrest him without solid proof. You know that."

"Relax, Sebastian," I said, voice smooth as cold espresso. "We're not arresting anyone… yet. We're observing. Let him make mistakes. That's how copycats behave. They *crave* attention."

He didn't respond. Just stared at me like he was trying to read a language he'd forgotten.

By afternoon, we were driving through Chandigarh's rain-slicked streets to Rajiv's apartment. Sector 37 smelled like wet concrete and stale chai. The kind of neighborhood where secrets hid behind curtains and peeling paint. The rain had turned the alleyways into veins of filth and runoff, the gutters gurgling like something alive.

Rajiv's building was a crumbling three-story block with rusted railings and a flickering stairwell bulb that buzzed like a dying insect. We climbed to the second floor, boots echoing on cracked tiles.

He opened the door after the third knock. Thin, pale, twitchy; exactly the sort of person everyone would believe could not be a copycat killer. His eyes darted between us like he was scanning for escape routes.

"I… I don't know why you're here, Ma'am…" he stuttered.

I smiled, tapping my pen. "Just routine questions, Rajiv. About Mahesh Khurana. Heard anything unusual?"

"No! Nothing! I… I mean… I just write about crimes, I… I—"

His apartment smelled like old paper and instant noodles. Walls lined with clippings, some yellowed, some fresh. Crime scene photos, headlines, red circles drawn around names. A shrine to violence. A scrapbook of obsession.

Sebastian stayed silent behind me, watching carefully. I could feel him calculating, doubting, trying to see through him. Cute.

I left Rajiv talking while I took mental notes. Nervous ticks, overemphasis on innocence, exaggerated gestures. Perfect. Everything I needed to believe he was capable of more than he was showing.

His fingers trembled when he reached for his tea. His voice cracked when I mentioned Mahesh's jaw. His eyes flicked to a drawer when I asked about knives.

I asked to use the bathroom. He hesitated. That was enough.

Inside, the sink was stained with rust. A razor blade sat on the edge, flecked with something dark. Not blood. Ink. Red ink. I pocketed it anyway.

Back in the Crime Branch, I mapped out Rajiv's routines and cross-referenced them with the timeline of the murder. The alignment wasn't perfect; but I didn't care. My notes would be interpreted by others as genius deduction, not creative misdirection.

I pinned his photo to the board. Drew lines. Created patterns. The illusion of clarity.

Sebastian finally confronted me in private, voice low: "Cyra, are you sure about this? Something feels… off about the way you're handling it. I'm worried about you."

I smiled, tapping my pen against my notebook. "Old man, you worry too much. It's all under control. I am fine."

But inside, I felt a chill.

Not fear. Not doubt.

The chill of art. Of manipulation. Of watching the city chase shadows while someone held the brush.

I stared at the board. At Rajiv's photo. At the red string that connected him to Mahesh, to the maid's testimony, to the grainy footage. It was beautiful. A web spun from suggestion and silence.

And somewhere in the back of my mind, the next canvas awaited. More elaborate, more deliberate, more… perfect.

Because this wasn't just a case.

It was a gallery.

And I was curating the show.

CHAPTER 5

The Canvas Deepens

Rain had turned Chandigarh into a reflection of neon puddles and wet asphalt. The city no longer felt like a place; it felt like a mood. Sector 8, near the PGI hospital back alleys, smelled of petrol, damp earth, and smoke from late-night tea stalls. That scent clung to your clothes and lingered in your nostrils long after you left. It was sharp, metallic, and somehow alive, like the city itself was breathing secrets. That was where the second body waited, and already the air felt heavier, thick with anticipation and malevolent artistry.

The victim this time was a woman. Mid-thirties, elegant, commanding even in death. *Ananya Mehta.* A lawyer whose reputation had been built on letting high-profile criminals walk free, whose smile had disarmed judges, journalists, and juries alike. She had defended politicians, gang leaders, corporate sharks. Her life had been a carefully staged performance. And now she was the ultimate irony, a performance paused and framed by someone who wanted the world to see her differently.

I crouched beside her, notebook in hand, the other hand gripping lukewarm coffee. Steam curled upward, mingling with the mist that clung low over the alley. The air smelled of wet cement, spilled petrol, and copper. Copper meant *blood*, and it was strong, metallic, clinging to my tongue as I inhaled.

She was posed in grotesque elegance. Arms arched over her head, elbows bent at sharp angles, fingers curved like a ballerina caught mid-dance. Her sari clung to her drenched body, darkened by the rain and flecked with crimson. Red roses had been tucked into the folds of the fabric. They were not scattered carelessly, but deliberately placed. Some petals pressed into her skin until they absorbed her blood, turning a dark shade of maroon. The folds of her sari made a frame around her wounds, almost theatrical in design.

I leaned closer and my stomach twisted at the next detail. Her mouth had been manipulated. Lips parted unnaturally, corners pulled back as if she were smiling at some unseen audience. Streaks of red lined her teeth, some dried, some wet. Her eyes were open, wide and staring into nothing, pupils dilated. The expression frozen on her face was not peace but terror meticulously curated. One of her earlobes had been pierced with a thorned rose stem, small punctures surrounding it, a subtle flourish only visible at a certain angle.

The torso was a gallery of calculated cruelty. Slash marks traced across her abdomen and chest, shallow but deliberate. They formed geometric patterns, lines framing the glyph inked into her skin. Some cuts were faint, almost imperceptible, others bled freely into the wet fabric. The scent of iron was stronger here. Her hands were smeared with streaks of blood, rubbed into the folds of her sari like macabre brush strokes. Her fingernails were chipped, some broken, stained with dark red. It felt as though the killer had taken the time to study her body before beginning the work, almost reverent in his method.

"Art," I whispered. "Every move calculated. Every fold deliberate. The killer's signature."

Sebastian appeared behind me, water dripping from his jacket, boots squelching against the wet pavement. "Cyra, you are saying that, like it is beautiful."

I glanced up at him, dark humor curling my lips. "Isn't it? Beauty and horror often walk together. They just happen to bleed a lot in between."

He did not respond. His gaze lingered on her, jaw tight, hands shoved into wet pockets. The constables remained at a careful distance, uneasy in the rain and in the presence of the body. One gagged quietly behind a dumpster. The roses were wilting fast, petals softening and bleeding deeper into her sari, merging with the crimson that already coated her skin.

Witnesses trickled in, anxious and hesitant, murmuring under the dim streetlights. A nurse on her smoke break, a ward boy dumping trash, each offering fragmented recollections. I guided them gently, like a conductor drawing a story out of reluctant instruments.

"Did you see anyone unusual?"

"Was she alone?"

"Did you hear anything strange, footsteps, voices, music?"

The fragments they offered were tantalizingly useless. A tall figure vanishing into the shadows, a rustling sound like plastic brushing stone, a faint trace of perfume carried on the rain. Nothing solid. Everything suggestive.

"This is escalating," Sebastian muttered, barely audible over the rain. "Pattern is clear now. Corrupt targets, meticulous execution. The copycat is stepping up."

I nodded, pen scratching across the paper. "Or someone who wants us to think there is a copycat. Someone hiding in plain sight."

His gaze lingered on me. "Cyra, you think too much sometimes."

I tapped my pen against my notebook. “No such thing as thinking too much. Only thinking too little is dangerous.”

The forensic team arrived, gloves snapping, kits clicking open like surgical trays. I watched them work, careful and precise. Swabbing, photographing, measuring every detail. One of them lifted the edge of the sari and froze, his hand trembling.

“Ma’am,” he called out. “You need to see this.”

Beneath the roses, etched into the skin of her abdomen, was a symbol. Not carved, not torn. Inked, as if the killer had brought a tattoo kit to the scene. A delicate spiral, surrounded by tiny dots, almost glowing against her pale skin. Ancient. Ritualistic. Purposeful.

Sebastian leaned in. “What the hell is that?”

“Not random,” I said, voice low. “It is a signature. A glyph. The killer is evolving.”

I traced the spiral with my gloved finger, careful not to touch the skin. The lines were precise, almost alive, a pattern that seemed to hum under the harsh alley lights. I could feel the intention, the patience, the obsession that had gone into this. The symbolism screamed: this was more than murder. This was performance.

The forensic report later confirmed what I suspected. Precise knife angles. Staged positioning. Meticulous care to avoid leaving identifiable traces. No fingerprints. No DNA. The roses were a new addition, a deliberate flourish. Whoever did this wanted a message, but only the right eyes would read it.

I went back to the Crime Branch, spreading both murder files across my desk. Mahesh Khurana and Ananya Mehta. Patterns were unmistakable. Corruption. Power. Public faces. Private sins. Subtle differences hinted at evolution. A new cruelty, a deeper theatricality, a greater understanding of fear and attention.

I adjusted timelines. Rewrote witness statements. Highlighted inconsistencies that pointed outward. The illusion of chaos. Only the keenest observer would see the threads I wove.

Sebastian's doubts sharpened like a blade pressing against my ribs. He did not know what he was holding against. Not yet.

He cornered me in the hallway later, voice low and urgent. "Cyra, this is not just another case. You are treating it like a performance."

I met his gaze. "Because it is."

He flinched. "You do not mean that."

I stepped closer. Fluorescent lights cast long shadows over us. "Every killer performs. Every victim is a stage. We choose whether to watch or to direct."

His eyes widened. Fear and disbelief flickered. "You are not just chasing the killer. You are curating them."

I did not deny it.

Later that night, I returned to my desk, maps and sketches sprawled across every inch of space. Two victims. Two masterpieces. And the world was chasing shadows.

I poured another cup of espresso. The bitterness grounded me, sharpened me. Dangerous? Perhaps. Exhilarating? Absolutely.

I opened my notebook to a fresh page. At the top, I wrote:

Canvas Three:

And left the rest blank.

Because the killer's canvas had only just begun. And I was already framing the next exhibit.

CHAPTER 6

Headlines and Hidden Hands

The sun tried and failed to break through the low, gray clouds over Sector 17 Plaza. The sky looked bruised. Even without full light, the city had been up for hours. Word traveled faster than traffic. Rumor fed off rumor. By the time I reached the Crime Branch headquarters in Sector 26 the plaza was already a stage set for other people's stories.

Reporters clustered like gulls outside the glass doors. Microphones extended on long, impatient arms. Camera crews jostled for angles. Phones glowed red with live feeds and breaking alerts. Laptops perched on car bonnets ran auto-updates that rewrote the evening a dozen different ways every minute. Thc air smelled of hot tar, old coffee and the faint metallic tang of rain that would not come. The noise had its own rhythm, a staccato of questions and the crack of flashbulbs.

I stood just inside the foyer, coffee cooling in my hand, pen tapping against a notebook. The tapping had become a ritual. It steadied me while everything else accelerated. Sebastian was less graceful but more constant at my shoulder. He watched the press like a man watching a slow-motion car crash, arms folded, coat still damp from the morning drizzle. He looked older in that light. The lines at his eyes deepened when he frowned.

"Cyra, do you really need to feed them this much?" he said. His voice was quiet, flat with an irritation that had nothing to do with cold.

I smiled without showing my teeth. "Old man, facts are facts. Spin is someone else's problem."

He did not laugh. He rarely laughs these days.

I stepped out into the press crush and the sound swelled like surf. The first microphones were aimed straight for my face. The same handful of reporters that always smelled a story first blocked the way, their questions short and sharp like jabs in the ribs.

"Sub-Inspector Singh! Is it true there is a copycat?"

"Is Rajiv Malhotra under arrest?"

"Are the murders connected to the Sculptor case from last year?"

I raised my hand. Control is a simple physical thing when the crowd respects authority. I did not always command it. When I did, the pleasure was steady and cold.

"We are pursuing all leads diligently," I said. My voice was even, practiced. "We have a suspect in connection with the Mahesh Khurana case and the subsequent attack on Advocate Ananya Mehta. Evidence is being verified. We urge the public not to speculate."

The pause stretched. Reporters lean into silence the way people lean into an oxygene blackout. They crave it because it forces someone to fill the empty space with certainty. I watched them bend forward, waiting for the story I already knew they wanted to write.

"Is there a copycat?" a reporter shouted, louder than the rest.

I tilted my head and let the weight of the moment sit on the words. "It is possible that someone is imitating the original killer. But we cannot confirm that at this time."

Seed planted. The world would run with it and not water it so much as set it on fire.

By evening the headlines had developed teeth. The news vans had parked their neon logos in a tight ring around the steps. Channels replayed my press statement in panels with scrolling barbs and animated graphics. The copycat theory rippled through social media. Opinion pieces declared me reckless or brilliant depending on the writer's appetite for drama. Message boards filled with a thousand half-formed theories. People tagged politicians, linked old court transcripts, and posted photos of roses from florists who had closed thirty minutes earlier.

Inside the office Sebastian watched the monitors with a jaw so tight it looked like a physical strain. He muttered, "You are too young to play with people like this."

"And yet here I am," I said, tapping the pen against the laminated evidence board until the sound became an obedient metronome.

After the storm of cameras came the slower, colder work. The press pack drifted away, each journalist carrying their version of truth like contraband. The office settled into the shuddering silence that follows any explosion of attention. I closed the glass door, cut the noise, and moved to my desk.

The crime maps fanned out across the table like a new continent. Pins, red and black, clustered and skated across sector lines. Timelines were layered on top of one another in a handwriting that grew more precise as the night deepened. Witness statements in folders smelled faintly of rain and cheap paper. Forensics reports sat in neat stacks. Security footage arrived on hard drives. Bodies of work assembled into the hollow museum of investigation.

I began to frame the narrative for the others. The media would take the narrative and sharpen it into a weapon or a shield. I preferred it as a tool. Narrative bends attention. Attention bends resources. Resources produce results. That was a brutal and useful arithmetic.

Rajiv Malhotra had become the face of the "copycat" in polite conversation. He had motive by virtue of past association, opportunity by virtue of proximity and time, and a public record that could be arranged to look increasingly incriminating with strategic emphasis and careful omissions. I moved pieces around the board in a deliberate choreography. A CCTV clip here with a suspiciously cropped timestamp. A witness recollection there, slightly rephrased to intensify memory of a man's build. An old misdemeanor note highlighted in a way that suggested pattern rather than accident.

It looked, from the outside, like deduction. From the inside it was architecture.

Sebastian hovered in the doorway. He did not step in. He watched me build. He watched me frame. When he finally spoke his voice was softer than the pen scratching on paper.

"Cyra, something about this does not feel right."

I let the pen hover, uncaring of the ink bead forming on the tip. "That is because it isn't about right or wrong, Sebastian. It is about control. And right now I control the narrative."

He did not answer. Let him stew. Let him learn that doubt can be an engine. Let him learn the weight of the silence I gave him.

The office emptied as midnight crept toward two in the morning. Lights dimmed, leaving pools of fluorescent glare and long, patient shadows. Forensics left with evidence boxes, the bags sealed tight. The reconstruction team had gone home, exhausted and hollow-eyed. I stayed. I always stayed.

I opened the coroner's file on my laptop and slid images across the screen, not for the press but for my own calibration. The photographs were clinical and brutal. Ananya Mehta's features had been arranged in that grotesque pose. The roses were still visible in close-ups, petals dark and sodden. The cuts on her torso were shallow in places and deeper in others, as if the killer had been testing the resistance of flesh. The glyph inked into her skin shone oddly against the pallor. The spiral and dots took on different meanings under different lights. It read like a language designed to be read by a certain kind of mind, an initiation token or the end of some private fable.

I zoomed. Each frame offered something new. The corner of the sari had a smear that looked like fingerprints in motion but then blurred. The fabric of the roses was threaded with fibers that forensic told me came from a very particular kind of florist wrap. The petals had traces of a chemical used in certain flower preservatives, a detail that could connect the killer to the marketplace at a particular hour. These were the kinds of threads only some people noticed. I made sure to point them out in passing when I needed the others to follow a trail that encouraged them away from other things.

News channels ran graphic cutaways alongside theorists and hot takes. They described wounds and staged poses with a breathless candor that made the city hungry for more images. Viewers commented in a monsoon of reaction.

Some were sickened. Some were excited. Many wanted to imagine the killer as a reflection of their own moral certainties. The internet does excellent work at turning horror into entertainment. That was why controlling the story mattered.

I watched one segment where an anchor spoke over a looping clip of roses being arranged. She used the word "masterpiece" and smiled in a way that made my skin crawl. Her voice tried to gamify the body into a spectacle. I made a note of the channel and the producer. They would be useful later. People who turn death into ratings can be nudged into specific narratives when the right pressure is applied.

At two thirty I walked down to the holding room. Rajiv Malhotra was not in custody yet, but his name polled the air like an accusation. I wanted to see what the precinct was hearing in whispers and to steer the whispers where needed. There was a packet on Malhotra in the evidence locker, quotes culled from his past interviews, a shaky alibi, an old complaint. I opened it with gloved hands and read fast, not for truth but for cadence. I jotted the phrases I could leverage. Language is a lever.

The station's holding area was a fluorescent rectangle smelling of disinfectant and stale sweat. The duty inspector gave me a look that rarely varied. He trusted procedure more than people. He handed over a witness statement from the nurse who had discovered Ananya's body. The handwriting was shaky. The words repeated themselves in small, nervous loops. She had been on a smoke break behind the PGI service road.

She had heard a sound like tissue rustling. She had seen a figure retreat. She had dropped her cigarette and run.

I adjusted the phrasing in my mental map. Rustling meant fabric. Fabric suggested a sari, a wrap, something culturally common and thus unremarkable in the crowd. Unremarkable is what reality loves best because it hides dangerous patterns.

A younger constable shuffled in with a file and sat across from me. His eyes refused to meet mine. He had been at the alley earlier, his boots still carrying a fine grit from the muck. “Ma’am,” he said, voice small, “someone from television called and asked for the autopsy photos. Wanted them for a feature.”

I felt a coldness expand, slow and precise. “Who called?”

“Number blocked,” he said. “They said they were doing a human interest piece.”

People who wanted the images did not want human interest. They wanted spectacle.

“Record the number and push for a subpoena,” I said. “We will need a paper trail.”

He scribbled and left, and the lights in the holding room hummed on. I stared at the blank walls and thought about the woman behind the roses and the inked spiral. The city was hungry for answers. It would eat bodies whole if given half a reason.

At three in the morning I sat alone at my desk and let the silence wrap around me. I imagined the headlines as hands, as claws. Hand after hand turned the city and its people into pages. People read, commented, and then moved on. The slow rot of attention is what allowed some things to persist in shadow. One could push and prod the attention like a child moving magnets on a refrigerator. The trick was making sure those magnets held the right pieces and the right distance apart.

In the quiet I began to plan the next move. If the world believed in a copycat, resources would be funneled toward a theory that might be false. If the theory held, then precious manpower would be directed at a single suspect who might be a convenient scapegoat. That would be fine, in some ways useful, if the true aim was to draw eyes off someone else, someone whose involvement could not yet be revealed without more preparation. That was the calculus I balanced against my conscience at night.

I made a list. It was a map of diversions and demands.

First, cultivate the narrative. Plant small leaks to the press at timed intervals. Let them build a motive for Malhotra that seemed plausible to the average reader. Highlight his ties to a florist who used that preservative. Make the timeline place him near Sector 8 on the night of the second murder in a way that read like proximity without proving causality. Let social outrage push for an arrest. The cry for quick justice would create space to control the exposure.

Second, watch the families. The relatives of victims are magnetic in media. They draw sympathy and they invite speculation. If the killers wanted attention, they would engineer a spectacle of grief. If they wanted to distract, they would exploit that spectacle to color public perception. I needed to be present when television cameras found them. My voice at those moments could cut a narrative thread or stitch a new one.

Third, monitor the supply chain. Flowers, wraps, preservatives. Where were the roses purchased? Which vendors could be traced? Which cameras could show purchases? The killer had introduced a motif. Motifs have supply lines. I would trace them until the thread soured for someone useful.

Fourth, keep Sebastian close even if he would not trust me. Distrust can be an advantage when the other person still carries authority and questions. I needed his honest skepticism on the surface and not his panic under it. Let him chew on doubts that left him raw and ineffective rather than furious and active.

I wrote the list in block letters on an evidence pad and left the pad face down on the desk. It was a promise to myself as much as a plan.

At dawn I walked to the window and watched the city wake. Vendors set up stalls. A woman with a stall of secondhand books arranged them like offerings. The headlines had children in them now, the kind that feed gossip columns. Shops closed in sympathy or in fear. The roses that had been mentioned in every broadcast popped up in photos of bouquets someone had sent to news anchors. No one was immune to the impulse to aestheticize grief.

When the morning shift arrived, the office filled with a new energy. Some of the people who had slept at their desks rose like zombies, hair askew, eyes unnaturally bright. A courier arrived with a stack of printouts from a florist near Sector 8. I opened them and pretended surprise at the similarities I claimed to discover. People like to be part of an unraveling mystery. It gives them the illusion of agency.

There were calls from politicians wanting reassurances. Calls from editors begging for exclusives. Messages from TV producers offering interview slots the next day. Each voice wanted narrative currency and confirmation that someone was in control. I sterilized answers into statements and released them at intervals. The drip-feed had to feel honest and measured or suspicion would leak into the air like steam.

By afternoon the newspapers had invented a stylized moniker for the killer. They called him the Sculptor in headlines that smudged seriousness into myth. It looked better in print than it deserved. My own actions may have fed the myth, but it was useful. People love stories with shapes. The story had become a beast and my hand at the glass fed it with careful morsels.

Even as the media devoured the plot, I kept watch for patterns that did not fit the public story. In a surveillance update I noticed a taxi driver who had looped past Sector 8 three times the night of the murder. Not an obvious link but a detail. I pulled the vehicle's license plate, then pulled driver registration and his travel logs. He had brought bouquets to a nursing home two days prior and had been paid in cash. Small things that could be tied together and then severed. Proof that could be shaped to point either way.

In the late afternoon Sebastian found me at the evidence board. Sunlight leaked through the blinds in thin bars. He looked exhausted and something tighter than doubt had settled on his face. He crossed to me and put a hand on the map where I had placed a red pin.

"You are playing with fire," he said.

"Fire is useful," I replied. "Fire purifies, clarifies. It draws out the things that hide best."

He stared at me for a long time. Then his jaw worked and he said, "If you are wrong, Cyra, innocent people will burn."

I met his eyes. "Then the wrong path will have cost me as well. I can lose. I accept that."

He did not look satisfied. The truth is the truth; it rarely comforts.

Night fell again. The city twinkled and the headlines refreshed and the world tuned in and turned away as if by some imperative of distraction. Somewhere, someone was preparing the next masterpiece and somewhere else someone else would be deciding what to wear to the funeral that had not yet been called. The angle I had set would shift time and attention and permit other hands to move unseen.

I turned the page of my notebook and wrote two words in a margin.

Canvas Three.

I folded the notebook closed and slid it into my drawer. The public would talk. The police would investigate. The media would fabricate. The killer would continue to work or rest or vanish. Somewhere in all of this, the truth waited like a splinter. It would hurt when I pulled it out, but I had learned that pain meant you were doing something.

Outside, the city breathed and shifted and pretended that by naming things it had understood them. Inside, hands moved quietly, rearranging small truths into a shape that could be carried. I lit a cigarette I did not mean to finish, and watched the smoke draw itself up and disappear into a sky that refused to give light.

If the world read headlines as truth then the headline was a hand. I intended to be the one that guided it.

CHAPTER 7

The Copycat's Trail

Rajiv Malhotra's apartment was the sort of place that kept its past on the top shelf like dust. Peeling paint traced lazy rivers down the walls. A ceiling fan spun slow and tired. The thin window barely kept out the traffic noise. The smell of old newspapers and instant chai hit me the moment I opened the door and stepped inside. There was a faint sweetness under the dust, as if someone had tried to hide something bitter with sugar.

He paced like a man trying to walk his way out of an accusation. His fingers fussed with the frames of his spectacles until the skin at the side of his nose glowed pale. Twitching hands, small gasps between sentences, eyes that kept darting toward the bookcase as if the books might rearrange themselves into an alibi.

Perfect. Exactly what the cameras would want to see when they filmed the interview later. Perfect for everyone who wanted a villain shaped like a stereotype.

"Good morning, Mr. Malhotra," I said, smooth as poured concrete. Pen ready, notebook open. "I am Sub-Inspector Cyra Singh. We are investigating the recent murders in Chandigarh. We have some questions for you."

He swallowed and his Adam's apple bobbed in a way that made me think of a bird startled on a branch. "I-I've done nothing," he stammered. "I write about crime. That is all. Nothing like this."

Sebastian hung back by the doorway, rain still beading on his coat from the drive over. He watched Rajiv with a kind of slow, dangerous curiosity. Every twitch Rajiv made seemed to register like a new variable in Sebastian's mind. His eyes flicked to me briefly, suspicion folded under concern, and then slid back to the man in the apartment.

I let Rajiv ramble while I wrote. Every overblown gesture, every tiny stutter and strained laugh were entries on the page. Later, those lines would be interpreted by other people as evidence rather than theatre. Later, someone else would nod and say smart things about motive and pattern while I watched how neatly the story fit the frame I had prepared.

"I write articles," Rajiv said. "I am fascinated by killers. I study them. Sometimes I fictionalize things to understand them. I never acted anything out."

His hands twisted in on themselves. The cuticles were ragged. He scratched a line into the air when he talked, drawing invisible threads that never joined into a coherent picture.

"You understand why you appear interesting to us," I said. I tilted my head and let the silence do some of the work. People feel compelled to fill empty space. They will confess everything or nothing. Both are useful.

He laughed, brittle, a sound that made the books on the shelf seem very heavy. "They always think writers are closer to the darkness. They always want someone to be the story. I never thought I would be the headline."

Sebastian moved. He stepped forward and asked the practical questions. Where were you the night of the 14th? Who can confirm you were at home? Do you have a record of purchases for that day? Each question landed like a measured tap on a window waiting for a reply.

Rajiv's answers fit a fragile structure. He had been home. He had ordered food. He had been working on a piece about ritual in modern crime. He mentioned florists in a sentence that hung oddly in the air as if he had not meant to say it out loud. "Roses are symbolic," he said. "People read symbols into anything these days."

I watched his face when he said roses. It tightened, then softened, as if he had felt something behind the word and decided to pretend he had always known it was safe to say.

After thirty minutes of peeling back layers, of watching the man perform himself into a corner, we left. Rajiv shut the door with hands that trembled for a beat longer than necessary. The corridor smelled of damp concrete and cigarette smoke. Sebastian exhaled, irritated.

"Cyra," he said while we stepped into the rain that had started again, "are you sure about this? You are guiding him. You are shaping the narrative. That is dangerous."

I shrugged and the motion was small and elegant. "Dangerous is subjective. For now we need him to be the visible suspect. Let the public and the media chase him. Meanwhile we will track the real artist quietly."

Sebastian's silence was a thing with edges. He did not trust me fully. Good. Let him doubt. Uncertainty keeps people predictable. Complacency is the enemy of control.

Back at the Crime Branch I layered Rajiv's alibi against the timelines from the two murders. The fit was almost precise. Close enough to be suspicious. Far enough to be defendable. A few small inconsistencies made the copycat angle believable, the sort of details that would look damning when framed in a certain light. I circled them lightly on my notes, made sure the emphasis was convincing. Planting evidence is not only about what you leave behind but also about what you edit out.

The first slip arrived in the form of a call slip from CFSL. A junior officer knocked and handed me a thin sheet of paper. Fingerprint results on the roses recovered from Ananya Mehta's body were inconclusive. Partial prints. Smudged ridges. Could belong to many people.

I tapped my pen and smiled faintly. Ambiguity is the engine of suspense. Ambiguity keeps the crowd leaning in. If everything screams certainty, attention collapses. If things undulate between possibility and danger, people keep watching.

Sebastian's voice came from the doorway where he had been listening. He sounded bluntly worried.

"Cyra, you are playing a game that can ruin lives. Be careful."

Careful tasted like metal to me.

"Careful is a boring word," I said. "I prefer art."

He did not answer beyond a look that suggested he would tally this night later in the ledger of mistakes and virtues alike.

I spent the next hours cross-checking. The roses, the florist wrap, the preservative traces. The partial prints were enough to suggest a link to a series of vendors who used the same kind of sulphate treatment on their stems. One florist in Sector 8 had a history of cash transactions and no formal invoices. Another delivery driver had CCTV footage showing a man with Rajiv's build near an alley the week before. Each thread was thin. Each, if tugged hard enough, could form the beginning of a rope.

I arranged these threads on the evidence board to look neat. A map with pins, a timeline with arrows. For the casual observer this looked like a precise deduction. For me it was architecture.

Then I pulled up the autopsy images again. I needed to remember why all of this mattered beyond theatre. Ananya Mehta had been left in an arrangement that was clinical in its composition and obscene in its tenderness. Roses tucked into her sari. Cuts on the torso fanning out like a fan of cruel fingers. A glyph delicate yet sinister etched into the skin of her abdomen. The killer's hand was careful with flesh and precise with blood. The body had been posed to make a point, to direct the eye. Anyone who made art like that needed either an audience or an instruction guide.

I had watched Ananya Mehta's face in the photos until the light faded from outside. The jaw slack. The mouth held in an unnatural smile. The petals had pressed into the skin until they warmed with blood. There was a scent I could almost conjure even looking at the images, copper heavy and floral, like someone had tried to perfume violence into beauty.

These images were why Sebastian worried and why the public would want a villain to fit neatly into a box. People want monsters they can identify. They are less comfortable with the idea that a monster chooses its time and its medium.

At midnight a junior analyst arrived with an update. "Ma'am, we have a taxi route that shows a vehicle circling Sector 8 the night of the second murder," he said. "Noted driver. Paid in cash for pickup near a flower distributor at 1:12 a.m."

I smiled like I was taking a photograph with my mind. Small confirmations that could be turned into lines of suspicion. A driver who made cash runs to flower stalls. Purchases of preservative-packed roses around the hours likely to have been used. Partial prints on petals. None of it conclusive on its own, but together they hummed like a chorus.

I fed these raw notes into the channels that would shape public appetite. A whisper to a journalist here, a casually remarked concern to a detective over tea there. Nothing illegal. Only curated implication. When the press seeded stories implying Malhotra's interest in ritual and his proximity to flower stalls, calls poured into the station. People want to point at faces and say you are the reason for my fear. The performance of accusation is a public service and a private satisfaction.

Rajiv's articles were easy to find. He wrote about the aesthetics of violence, about the ways the media hungered for the ritualistic. He romanticized killers in careful paragraphs that never crossed into endorsement. He wrote about symbols and meaning and the way words can shape culpability. That writing became my ledger. I emphasized certain lines in internal memos and underemphasized others. Context is a kind of talisman. You can protect or curse with the way you set it in place.

At three in the morning I pulled the CFSL printouts back up. Partial prints meant nothing unless I funneled them into a narrative. I asked the analysts to run enhancement routines, to check for chemical treatments that might skew ridge patterns. They worked late, eyes ringed black, fingers moving fast. In the end the prints had a match probability that sat uncomfortably in the middle. It suggested movement without committing to identity. I liked the space that uncertainty created.

Sebastian returned once more to my desk, hands in his coat pockets, his voice softer than before. "If you push him too far, Cyra, and he snaps, then you will have made the line between planner and execution impossible to follow."

I met his eyes and for a moment I thought he would see something in me that I preferred hidden. "If he snaps, he will do it for his own reasons," I said. "If he does not, then someone else remains the artist. Either outcome reveals more than standing still."

He shook his head and walked away with the slow, heavy motion of a man who carries a weight that is not always his own to shoulder.

In the blackout hours between night and dawn I sat with the smell of stale coffee and the fatigue that hums in bones after truth bending. I thought of the man who had posed the bodies. Skill and madness can be cousins. Both dress in meticulous habit. Both can learn the same movements until what is normal is only what they have repeated.

The copycat scenario had value. It would agitate the public for a quick resolution. A suspect with a past in the public eye is a tidy answer for the terrified. It would also do something else. It would give me a cover. While everyone crowded around the man on stage, the true artist might move freely. Patterns could be watched without the glare. Movements could be tested without panic. Attention is both a sword and a shield. I had spent enough nights learning how to hold it in my hands without cutting myself.

Dawn found me still at my desk, a thin strip of light cutting across the evidence board and making the pins glitter. I wrote a list of immediate tasks, careful with language, careful with the weight of suggestion. Trace florist supplies. Interview cash customers at the distributor. Pull the taxi driver's phone records and cross reference with known flower runs. Obtain surveillance for the alley behind the PGI service road at specific hours. Create small controlled leaks to the press to reinforce the copycat theory without locking us into a single conclusion.

In the margin of my notebook I wrote a single line and then underlined it twice.

Canvas Three.

It was not a prediction. It was a map. The phrase felt like a finger pressed into the wet clay of something that would later harden into a shape. The pattern was forming. A trajectory of scent and petals and blood. A trail with gaps intended to lure the wrong shoes.

Before I left I walked past the holding area. Rajiv's profile was silhouetted against a small window as he sat on a plastic bench. He looked smaller in the harsh fluorescent light than he had in his apartment. His hands were empty. His face had the exhausted look of a man who had been seen and not found.

I felt a tiny knot of something I could not name. Guilt perhaps, or a muted regret for the lives caught in the design. I folded it away like a receipt and put it in a drawer. Some debts are paid in evidence and some are paid in consequence. I was both willing and not willing to cash the check.

Outside the building the city breathed and rose and pretended that news was the same as truth. People would read and react and then, in a day or two, move on to the next vivid thing. The copycat story would hold attention long enough for certain doors to be opened and others to be closed. It would not be clean. Nothing involving blood and intent ever is. But it would be useful.

As I shut down my computer and gathered my notes, Sebastian appeared at the door. We did not speak. We did not need to. We had both memorized the shapes of the night and the ways a story can be guided to fit into a frame. We had both seen how headlines could be hands and how hands could hold the right knife.

I stepped into the rain and let it wash the city clean for a while. The petals of roses folded and unfurled in my mind like little flags. Somewhere the artist would be tracing the next line, considering which wound to show and which to conceal. I walked on, the trail behind me a thin line in the mud, the copycat theory humming in the air like a promise that could be fulfilled or revoked.

Either way, the canvas would deepen.

CHAPTER 8

Blood and Roses

It was late, past midnight, when the call came in. The voice on the line trembled, cracking against the static. "Ma'am… another body… Sector 14… abandoned textile warehouse…"

I drained the last dregs of coffee, the bitter warmth grounding me, and grabbed my notebook. My pen tapped against the dashboard as Sebastian drove through Chandigarh's rain-slick streets. The city's neon lights reflected in puddles like fractured constellations. Sector 14 smelled of rust, wet brick, and oil — a stench that seemed to cling to your skin. Perfect for a scene no one would stumble upon by accident. Perfect for someone who wanted to be noticed without being caught.

The warehouse loomed, a hulking carcass of brick and steel. Broken windows glinted like watchful eyes in the dim streetlight. Doors hung open on splintered hinges. Inside, the smell hit first — iron tang of blood, rot, and chemicals long abandoned by workers. The kind of scent that makes a person's stomach knot, makes a mind sharpen without realizing it.

The victim waited like a grim centerpiece. Judge Arvind Khanna, mid-50s, retired but infamous for clearing high-profile criminals, lay sprawled on the cracked concrete floor. His body was a statement. Arms outstretched as if embracing the ceiling, head tilted backward, eyes frozen wide in silent accusation. The red roses circled him like a morbid crown. Petals soaked in rainwater, some bruised, some torn by careful hands, dripping with rivulets of blood that gleamed under the sparse light. The floor around him was slick, a dark mirror reflecting the grotesque arrangement.

I crouched close, notebook open, pen poised. The faint smell of copper and wet fabric hit me like a visceral reminder of the body's reality. "Pattern confirmed," I whispered. "Each victim… selected carefully. Each pose… deliberate. Each signature… evolving."

Sebastian stepped beside me, rain sliding down his jacket in streams. "Cyra… you call this pattern 'art'? This is…" He shook his head, unable to finish the thought. I didn't blame him. He never could see it the way I did.

I smiled faintly, tapping my pen against my notebook. "It's a narrative, Sebastian. The world wants stories. We just provide them."

The constables lingered at the edges of the warehouse, uneasy, hands hovering over holsters, eyes wide as they took in the scene. I let them. This wasn't just about discovery. This was about control. About perception. About setting the tone for everyone who came afterward, including the press, the public, and, eventually, the killer.

I crouched closer, examining the victim. The cuts on his torso were not random. They fanned outward like cruel fingers, shallow on some areas, deep on others, each precise, deliberate, meant to draw the gaze along a path. The roses were not scattered—they were positioned with care, petals pressed against skin until blood and water mixed into a dark, intoxicating stain. His hands were positioned unnaturally, the fingers curved in silent accusation, like an orchestra conductor frozen mid-motion.

I bent lower, noting the glyph on his abdomen, a spiral etched in the flesh with surgical precision. Tiny dots circled the symbol, each one spaced evenly, almost invisible in the low light. The killer's signature was evolving. The glyph wasn't just a mark; it was a message for anyone who could read it. A language written in pain, in control, in quiet obsession.

Sebastian crouched beside me reluctantly, hands in his pockets, watching. "Cyra… look at this. It's… clinical. But it's escalating. Someone is becoming reckless."

I shook my head slightly, dark humor curling my lips. "Or meticulous. Escalation doesn't mean sloppiness. It means evolution."

He studied me, eyes narrowing in the faint, flickering light. "You've seen patterns like this before, haven't you?"

I laughed softly, tapping my pen against the desk in my mind as I scanned the scene. "Old man, patterns are everywhere. You just have to know where to look. And sometimes… you just have to create them yourself."

I moved around the body slowly, tracing the edges with gloved hands, careful not to disturb the evidence. The petals had been pressed in a circle at exactly one arm's length from the torso. One of the roses rested between the judge's fingers, its stem broken neatly, blood smeared across the petals. Tiny droplets dotted his shoes, his robes, even the cracked concrete. The edges of the glyph were almost imperceptibly raised, as if the killer had burned the symbol into the skin with a method I could only imagine.

I inhaled slowly. The metallic tang of blood mixed with the scent of wet roses created a heady perfume, the kind that lingers in memory. This scene wasn't random. Every detail was chosen. Every position deliberate. Every drop of blood a punctuation mark.

I crouched lower, notebook open. "Note placement of flowers, spacing, positioning of limbs. Note glyph and wounds. Signature evolving. Include rainfall impact on petals and blood pooling. Observe potential narrative for media consumption and public perception."

Sebastian's voice broke my concentration. "Cyra… you're too focused on theatrics. The killer is escalating. The risk is increasing."

I looked up at him, eyes glinting. "Risk is relative. Chaos is expected. Narrative is everything."

He studied me closely, seeing what he refused to name. "And if someone dies under your narrative? What then?"

I let silence answer. Silence was sharper than words. The constables shifted uneasily, as if hearing the question in their own skulls.

I walked around the warehouse, glancing at rusted machinery and broken looms. The shadows of old textile frames stretched across the floor, forming jagged lines that made the body seem like it floated in a frozen theater of horror. The echo of dripping water punctuated the silence. Somewhere a rat scurried, its tiny squeak swallowed by the empty cavern.

I crouched by the roses, gently brushing a fingertip across a petal coated in blood. The texture was slick and cool, the veins of the petals darkened almost black. The smell of copper intensified. I imagined the killer's hands arranging each bloom, fingers slick, precise, deliberate. Each petal a brushstroke, each wound a line in a story only he could read.

I glanced at Sebastian. "Notice the positioning. Arms straight, head tilted, eyes wide. The victim becomes a narrator. The body speaks, but only to those who know the language. Everyone else sees only terror."

He swallowed, uneasy. "Cyra… you… you analyze like this, but…" He shook his head. "It's horrifying."

I smiled faintly, pen tapping against my notebook. "Horrifying is part of the story. Fear is part of the art. The world hungers for it."

I documented every detail, from blood streaks on concrete to the faint impressions of shoes where the killer had moved. Tiny bits of fabric caught on jagged edges of steel. Water had formed puddles that reflected the fluorescent flicker of a distant streetlamp. I even noted the faint scent of perfume lingering near the doorway, the kind used to announce presence without sound.

Security footage from nearby warehouses was spotty. Shadows moved like wraiths. Nothing clear, nothing definitive. But it was enough to place Rajiv Malhotra in proximity if someone wanted to spin the narrative. A few frames of a man vaguely resembling him. A delivery van parked nearby, lights off. Enough to suggest involvement without committing.

Back at the Crime Branch, the timeline crystallized further. Mahesh Khurana, Advocate Ananya Mehta, now Judge Arvind Khanna. Three victims. Corruption, power, and escape from justice as a theme. Public attention skyrocketed. Social media buzzed with speculation. Rajiv's name appeared in whispers in newsrooms, online comment threads, and casual conversations. Perfect.

Sebastian's voice cut through my focus. "Cyra… the theatrics are fine, but the killer is escalating. Someone is taking bigger risks, leaving more evidence. This is dangerous."

I leaned back in my chair, tapping my pen against the wood. "Or meticulous," I said. "Each new move is deliberate. Evolution, not carelessness."

I pulled up the autopsy images again. The judge's eyes stared blankly at me, pupils dilated, frozen in accusation. The cuts fanned across his chest like cruel fingers. Each incision precise, a calculation. The glyph etched into his skin glimmered faintly under the camera flash, as if mocking the world for not understanding it. Petals pressed into the flesh left subtle bruises. Blood mingled with rainwater, forming intricate, temporary patterns on the concrete.

I let the images sink in. Skill and madness are often cousins. Both dress in meticulous habit. Both can learn the same movements until what is normal is only what they have repeated.

The thrill pulsed inside me. Creation. Control. Watching the world chase shadows while the true hand moved unseen. Another sip of coffee, another tap of the pen. The killer's canvas was spreading across Chandigarh. And I was the only one who truly knew its boundaries.

The night crept on, cold and wet, as I traced the path of petals, of footprints, of shadow. Somewhere, the artist was planning, sketching the next tableau. And I would be there to see it unfold, to frame it, to understand it before anyone else.

Canvas Four.

I wrote the words in my notebook, underlining them twice. Not a prediction. Not a warning. A map. A trajectory. A thread of blood and roses, of patterns and shadows, weaving through the city.

Outside, Chandigarh slept uneasily under the rain. Neon flickered like dying stars. Somewhere, a pair of hands arranged the next display. And the world would watch.

CHAPTER 9

Headlines, Hysteria, and Handprints

By morning, Chandigarh had transformed. The streets hummed like an anxious heartbeat, the air thick with humidity and rumor. Newspapers screamed with bold fonts, online portals erupted in pop-ups and push notifications, and television anchors debated endlessly, their voices clipped and sharp:

"Sculptor or Copycat? The City's Fear Grows"

"Judge, Lawyer, Businessman: Who's Next?"

"Pattern Emerges in Ritualistic Murders — Is the Copycat Close?"

I sipped my cold espresso, pen tapping lightly against my notebook, the sharp taste a reminder that control is a flavor best savored slowly. Every headline, every speculative opinion, every panel discussion had been seeded carefully. A story left to blossom in chaos. The world was chasing shadows, clinging to them like life preservers. Perfect.

Sebastian appeared in the doorway, coat still dripping from the drizzle outside, eyes narrowed and dark under his thick brows.

"Cyra… you've gone too far. The media's spinning this out of control. People are panicking."

I looked up, a faint smile tugging at the corner of my lips. "Old man, panic is attention mismanaged. Let them speculate. We don't control the narrative — we just decide which version of reality they get." My pen tapped rhythmically against the notebook, a metronome marking the city's pulse.

Rajiv Malhotra, the copycat suspect, had retreated into isolation. Perfect. Fear was his companion, and I could manipulate it without ever touching him. A text "accidentally" leaked to a journalist hinted at his nervous energy. A shadowy figure "seen" loitering near his apartment created whispers among online sleuths.

Nothing overt, everything plausible. His mind was a marionette, dancing to strings he could not see.

Inside the Crime Branch, I orchestrated the evidence like a conductor over a sinister symphony. Partial fingerprints, slightly misaligned timelines, blurry security footage; all pointing subtly at Rajiv, while the true path of the killer remained buried beneath layers only I could decipher. Every planted inconsistency was a breadcrumb for the unwitting to follow, a misdirection painting a perfect narrative of culpability.

Sebastian hovered behind my desk, his presence a shadow pressing against the edges of my carefully curated reality. "Cyra… you're too calm. Something about this doesn't sit right."

I looked up, pen tapping the edge of the notebook. "Calm? No. I'm exhilarated. This is the art of control, Sebastian. The thrill isn't in chasing the truth. It's in knowing that everyone believes they are chasing it… while it is already in your hands."

The city beyond the glass moved on obliviously. Pedestrians stepped around puddles without noticing the reflections of themselves in neon-smeared water. Buses rattled over wet asphalt, horns cutting through drizzle and the buzz of early chatter. Coffee stalls opened for the morning rush, the scent of roasted beans and fried snacks competing with the lingering tang of the previous night's rain. The murders had become a spectacle. The headlines were the gallery. The frightened public, the audience. And I… the unseen artist, pulling the strings.

I turned my attention back to the timelines. The first murder, Mahesh Khurana, posed like a fallen king with arms outstretched and the signature glyph faintly etched across his wrist. Ananya Mehta, mid-30s lawyer, displayed roses pressed into her sari and the spiral glyph inked across her abdomen. And now, Judge Arvind Khanna, arms spread wide, eyes wide in accusation, petals pressed into bruised flesh, blood pooled like wet velvet around him. Each scene, precise, deliberate, calculated to send a message only perceptible to those who knew how to read it.

I annotated the timelines, tracing every movement of the suspected copycat, marking security camera blind spots and alibi gaps. Partial fingerprints I had subtly highlighted in internal memos. Slight discrepancies in witness statements were circled and coded. Shadowy footage was placed side by side with open-source photographs of Rajiv Malhotra walking the streets days before the murders. Plausible, damning, impossible to disprove to anyone not paying attention to the subtext.

Sebastian's concern lingered behind me, pressing like the storm clouds outside. "Cyra… the escalation is real. The killer isn't just leaving messages anymore. They're daring someone to see the truth. Are you certain about Rajiv?"

I didn't answer immediately. Silence, carefully measured, stretched the room. My pen traced circles in the margin of my notebook, a tactile metronome against the tension.

"I never claimed certainty," I said finally, voice quiet but deliberate. "I claim control. Certainty is for fools who think fear can be contained."

The images from the autopsies and crime scenes flashed in my mind. Blood spattered in precise patterns. Petals bruised into the skin like signatures of intimacy and cruelty. Glyphs, etched or tattooed with meticulous intent. The killer's hand had an elegance to it, a terrifying sense of choreography. Each death was more than murder; it was a performance designed to invoke awe, terror, and obsession.

Outside, the rain had stopped but left streets slick, reflective, a mirror world where neon signs appeared fractured and multiplied. Somewhere, someone walked carefully, tracing paths, considering angles. Somewhere, the real killer was deciding on the next tableau. And I could imagine it all, line by line, stroke by stroke, before it happened.

I tapped my pen again, mapping connections between victims and public perception. The city's hysteria was an asset. Rumors spiraled into fear, fear into speculation, speculation into media frenzy. Each tweet, each news story, each whispered conversation was another brushstroke on a canvas only I could see in full.

The copycat angle worked perfectly. Rajiv Malhotra stayed confined, isolated, hesitant, feeding my narrative without knowing. Any slip he made; a hurried text, a nervous call; was amplified, recorded, and woven into the tapestry. His fear was a tool. His paranoia, a mirror for the public's imagination.

By nightfall, I returned to my desk, lamp casting a halo of dim light over the chaotic spread of papers, maps, timelines, and photographs. My coffee had cooled, but I barely noticed. I traced connections again, adding subtle tweaks: a shadow here, a fingerprint there, a slight misalignment in a timeline. Everything plausible, everything misleading. Precision masked as accident. Misrepresentation hidden in plain sight.

Sebastian's presence was a quiet hum behind me, the concern never leaving his eyes.

"Cyra… this is beyond manipulation. You're shaping hysteria, not investigating."

I didn't look up. My fingers traced a thin line connecting flower vendors, security blind spots, and Rajiv's movements.

"Hysteria is the medium," I said, voice soft but absolute. "Perception is the paint. Fear is the brush. And we… we control the strokes."

The thrill pulsed through me like a second heartbeat. Another canvas awaited. Bigger. Bolder. Perfect. Every planted handprint, every shadowy hint, every insinuation carefully measured. The city believed it was following the truth. In reality, it was following a story I had already written.

Outside, Chandigarh murmured in its oblivious rhythm. Neon flickered across puddles. Buses rattled. People argued over breakfast. Somewhere, news anchors debated the copycat theory, their energy feeding the narrative. Somewhere, a man sat alone, checking the news, wondering if he had done too much, too little, or just enough.

I leaned back, tapping my pen one last time. The coffee was cold, the ink on the page fresh. The thrill of creation wrapped around me, a velvet cloak stitched with shadows and intent. The next victim, the next message, the next canvas; it awaited in the mind of the artist. And I was already framing it in my imagination, ready for the city to see.

I wrote a single phrase in my notebook, underlining it twice:

Canvas Four.

A map. A trajectory of petals, blood, fear, and illusion. The pattern was forming. The city's hysteria was mine to sculpt. And the real artist was still moving unseen, painting the next masterpiece in silence, leaving only breadcrumbs for the unwitting to follow.

Chandigarh slept, unaware that every headline, every whisper, every heartbeat had already been choreographed. And I… I was that conductor.

CHAPTER 10

Too Close to Home

The rain had stopped, but the streets of Chandigarh glistened like wet glass, neon reflections fracturing across puddles, illuminating cracked sidewalks and forgotten alleyways. The city felt restless, like a creature waking from a storm.

I walked through Sector 26 Police Lines, notebook in hand, coffee warming my fingers, pen tapping with rhythmic urgency against the leather cover. The rhythmic click of Sebastian's boots behind me was the only other sound, his presence a constant shadow, eyes flicking across the maps I had spread across the table.

Every line, every arrow, every red dot represented movement, timing, and opportunity. The city had become a puzzle I could almost see in three dimensions. And now, it would soon add another piece.

The call came suddenly, sharp and tremulous over the phone line. "Ma'am… Sector 9… senior officer… body discovered in his home… deceased. Retired, highly respected… renowned for cracking high-profile corruption cases…"

I felt that familiar thrill coil in my stomach, a mixture of apprehension and excitement. This wasn't just another victim. This wasn't just a continuation of a pattern. This was personal. Too close.

I slipped into my rain-damp coat, pen tucked behind my ear, notebook ready. Sebastian followed silently, his face tight with concern.

The drive through wet, glistening streets was tense. Streetlights flickered in puddles, and trash cans spilled their contents over sidewalks, swept by the remnants of the storm. Somewhere, a stray dog barked, its voice swallowed by the echoing drizzle in the alleys.

The house in Sector 9 was deceptively quiet, almost serene in its suburban calm. Lawns trimmed, flowerbeds manicured, windows reflecting the gray sky. Inside, the smell hit immediately: polished wood, faint cologne, and an undertone of iron, subtle but undeniable. *Blood.*

The scene was precise. Surgical. Every item in the living room arranged exactly as though a curator had guided the hand of death. The retired officer's body was seated in his armchair, head tilted slightly forward, eyes open but glassy, hands folded across his lap. The red roses lay in perfect arcs around him, petals darkened where the rain from the night before had mingled with blood. The contrast of the softness of the flowers and the cold finality of death was arresting.

I crouched beside the body, notebook open, pen tapping against the page. "Patterns evolve, Sebastian," I whispered. "The killer wants the world to notice. And they do."

Sebastian's gaze swept the room, scanning walls, bookshelves, picture frames. "Patterns? Or someone is showing off? Someone who knows our routines… our weaknesses…"

I let the words hang. Dark humor tugged at my lips. "You worry too much. Patterns are neutral. It's the observer who decides the meaning."

The faint scent of roses mixed with iron and the polished wood of the furniture, a scent that seemed to linger like a question unanswered. I noted every detail, every subtle trace that could hint at the killer's process. The angle of the chair, the position of the hands, the placement of petals on polished oak. Blood pooled only in small, intentional rivulets, a crimson river carefully guided. No fingerprints. No stray DNA. Nothing left to chance. The precision was impossible, inhuman, and terrifying.

Sebastian crouched beside me reluctantly, eyes scanning the glyphs faintly etched into the officer's wrist; tiny, intricate spirals, etched in such a way that they could almost go unnoticed if someone didn't know what to look for. The signature of the artist. The evolution of the narrative.

"This is… beyond anyone's expectations," he murmured, voice tight. "It's escalating too fast. Too deliberate. This… this is personal."

I scribbled notes, tapping the page lightly. "Personal, yes. But only because it has proximity. The rest? Pattern. Signature. Narrative. Art, Sebastian. Art and fear entwined."

He studied me sharply. "And you… you call this art?"

I tilted my head, pen hovering above the paper. "Control, Sebastian. Precision. Storytelling. You see horror, I see choreography. You see terror, I see narrative. The eyes of the observer make the difference."

The forensics at CFSL confirmed what I already suspected. Wounds precise, calculated. No stray fingerprints, no DNA except the victim's own. The roses, carefully placed, as if by a hand both reverent and cruel. The signature intact. Escalation undeniable. Whoever this was, they were testing the boundaries. Whoever this was, they were close enough to touch the edges of our lives and still remain unseen.

Back at the Crime Branch, I began subtly planting ideas in the minds of my colleagues. Casual remarks here, a suggested scenario there, questions about inside knowledge and access. Rajiv Malhotra, the copycat suspect, was perfect for this. A narrative of inside information, proximity, and fear. Small hints, easy to believe, easy to follow. The public would latch onto them. The media would spin them. And the real trail, hidden beneath layers of carefully arranged chaos, remained mine alone to see.

Sebastian pulled me aside later, voice low, hesitant. "Cyra… you've seen this before. How do you recognize these details so quickly?"

I met his gaze, tapping my pen against the leather of my chair. "Experience, intuition… and maybe a little obsession."

He studied me, unease shadowing his features. "Cyra… be honest. Are you seeing connections others aren't… or creating them?"

I smiled faintly, dark humor curling at the edges of my lips. "Sometimes, Sebastian… the line between seeing and creating isn't so clear. Isn't that what makes the truth interesting?"

He didn't answer. Good. Let him stew in doubt. Let him question himself before he questions me. Let him worry about shadows while I traced their shapes.

The night deepened around the city. The map of victims sprawled across my desk: businessman, lawyer, judge, now officer. Each connected by invisible threads, each positioned carefully, each signature evolving. The thrill pulsed inside me like an electric current. Patterns, narratives, choreography. And all of it dancing just out of reach of those too literal to see.

I traced the paths slowly, deliberately, imagining the killer moving through the city: streets glistening from rain, shadows folding into corners, silent hands placing roses with perfect arcs, carving glyphs with calculated patience. I imagined the fear of the city, the obsession of the public, and the tentative panic of the copycat suspect, all manipulated by subtle nudges I had made hours, days ago.

Every flower, every drop of blood, every frozen expression was a letter in a story only I could read. And I could already anticipate the next chapters, the next positions, the next signatures.

Outside, Chandigarh breathed and moved obliviously. Pedestrians stepped over puddles, taxis rattled down neon-lit streets, and somewhere, a child kicked a stray ball that rolled through a deserted alley, missing bloodied petals by mere inches. Somewhere, the killer watched. Somewhere, the copycat trembled. Somewhere, the public whispered in fearful speculation.

Sebastian remained a shadow behind me, tight-lipped and wary. His eyes flicked repeatedly to the door as though expecting the world to intrude upon the careful architecture I had built. But for now, I was untouchable. Every narrative under control, every perception guided. Every whisper, every clue, every planted suspicion… mine.

I tapped my pen one last time, tracing a line between the latest victim and the previous three. The thrill tightened, a coil ready to spring. The game had changed. The copycat still moved blindly, unaware that his every move was already part of a story he could not influence. The public still obsessed, hungry for fear. Sebastian still suspicious, but blind to the truth.

For now, the canvas was mine. And the masterpiece… had only just begun.

CHAPTER 11

Framing Shadows

Rajiv Malhotra had become predictably erratic. Every jittery text, every trembling phone call, every nervous glance he cast around his apartment was a word in the story I was writing. My nudges were invisible, subtle as the shift of shadows at dusk. A casually dropped hint, a misfiled paper, a shadow vaguely captured on

CCTV; and he reacted exactly as I intended. Perfectly.

The morning light seeped through the Crime Branch windows, muted and streaked from last night's rain. I sipped coffee, letting its bitterness sharpen my senses. My pen tapped rhythmically against the notebook like a heartbeat I alone could hear, a metronome of intent. Sebastian lingered behind, arms crossed, eyebrows furrowed as he reviewed the city-wide timelines displayed on the screen. Every movement of every suspect, every minor inconsistency, every fleeting incident was meticulously plotted.

"We need to recheck timelines, movements, everything," I said casually, voice smooth, even playful. My words were both suggestion and command, planting ideas without revealing intention. I already knew the path the investigation would take.

Sebastian's gaze flicked up sharply. "Cyra… he's a journalist. How are we letting him slip into this narrative? People could get hurt if we mislead." His voice was low, cautious, threaded with unease.

I smiled faintly, pen poised above the page. "It's already too late for that. Everyone loves a scapegoat. We just make it convincing." Calm. Precise. Controlled. Every word, measured. The thrill pulsed beneath the surface, subtle but undeniable.

By mid-morning, we were on our way to Rajiv's apartment in Sector 37. The building loomed gray and peeling, rust creeping along railings like veins. The stairwell smelled of damp concrete and mildew, tinged faintly with the scent of old newspapers. Perfect for a stage of panic and dread.

Rajiv opened the door before we could knock. His body was taut, eyes wide, skin pale. “Ma’am… I didn’t…” His voice cracked, trembling like thin ice over water.

I leaned against the doorframe, pen tapping lightly against my notebook. “It’s not what you did, Rajiv… it’s how it looks.” The words hung between us, soft but lethal, precise as a scalpel.

His gaze flicked between Sebastian and me, eyes darting in panic. Every flinch, every hesitant gesture, every micro-expression; gold. His panic was not fear of the truth; he had no idea; but fear of the narrative I had created. Perfect.

The apartment smelled of stale chai, paper, and anxiety. A faint metallic tang of fingerprints clung to doorknobs and light switches. I watched as he wrung his hands, fingers trembling, knuckles whitening. Every twitch, every rapid blink, every shallow breath became part of my silent observation. Later, these signs would be interpreted as evidence of guilt.

I let him ramble, taking careful notes, letting him feel he was defending himself. His denials, stammering, and frantic attempts to justify himself were music. I didn’t need the truth; I needed the performance.

Small planted clues from weeks ago were now alive: the misfiled document left intentionally in his drawer, the faint shadow “captured” on security footage I had reviewed at leisure, the fingerprint “found” on a rose petal from an earlier crime scene. Each piece reinforced the narrative: Rajiv Malhotra was the copycat, the visible villain in a story I orchestrated.

Back at the branch, I meticulously mapped his movements against the murders' timelines: the coffees he bought, the buses he took, the fleeting interactions with neighbors. Minor inconsistencies, small errors, each highlighted subtly in the public-facing report. To any casual observer, the patterns aligned perfectly. To me, it was art.

Sebastian lingered, unease coiling in silence. His gaze flicked from the screens to me repeatedly, his frown deepening. "Cyra," he said finally, voice low, "you've never been this… precise. It's like you know the killer personally."

I allowed my smile to linger, dark and unreadable. "Maybe I do, Sebastian. Maybe I just understand what the city wants to see."

My thrill pulsed beneath my calm exterior. The city believed in shadows, in fear, in guilt. And I provided it in exactly the measure they desired.

By evening, DSP Sharma approved the preliminary arrest of Rajiv Malhotra. The media exploded. Headlines screamed across portals and TV screens:

"Copycat Captured? Police Question Journalist Suspected in Sculptor Murders"

"Rajiv Malhotra in Custody: Chandigarh Breathes a Sigh of Relief"

"Copycat Mystery Solved? Investigation Continues"

I tapped my pen against the desk. Coffee long gone cold. Everyone thought the case was moving forward. Everyone except me.

Because the real artist remained free. Silent. Watching. Thrilled by the chaos my subtle orchestration had wrought. Rajiv was the scapegoat, the red herring, the actor on the stage of my making. The city believed the narrative. The media believed it. Sebastian observed, suspicion forming, but incomplete. And the true killer? Still moving unseen through shadows, sculpting the next masterpiece.

I revisited the timeline, tracing streets, alleys, cafés; everywhere Rajiv had been; matching them against the victims' locations. Each step he took reinforced the narrative of guilt. Every glance over his shoulder, every nervous pause at street corners; all part of my silent orchestration.

Then I allowed myself a small indulgence: reviewing the photographs of past victims. Mahesh Khurana, posed stiffly. Ananya Mehta, limbs curved unnaturally, petals pressed into her sari, blood blooming into the fabric. Judge Arvind Khanna, seated in an armchair, hands folded, eyes wide, staring at unseen justice. Each signature, each careful positioning, each subtle glyph of blood was a letter in a story only I could read. The artistry thrilled me. I could almost see the hands of the killer moving, almost hear the careful placement of petals, the whispered calculations.

Sebastian lingered nearby, watching. He sensed something but couldn't grasp it. His unease grew like a storm cloud, threatening to burst, but he remained tethered to the narrative I had created. Perfect. Let him stew. Let him wonder. Let him chase shadows while the real hand moved unseen.

I tapped my pen against the desk, tracing invisible lines across the city map. Each victim's location, each timeline discrepancy, each planted clue was a note in a symphony of perception. The thrill was not in catching the killer; the thrill was in shaping reality itself, in orchestrating panic, in deciding what the city would believe.

The night deepened outside, streets slick with rain, neon lights reflected in puddles like fractured constellations. Somewhere, a stray dog barked. Somewhere, a child kicked a ball down an alley, oblivious to the petals stained with blood from earlier scenes. Somewhere, Rajiv trembled alone, reading headlines that I had curated for maximum impact. And somewhere, the real killer moved silently through the city, sculpting the next scene, thrilled by my orchestration, unaware that the city's attention had been entirely misdirected.

I leaned back, pen hovering, tracing the veins of thought across my notebook. Each line connecting victims, timelines, and suspects stretched like living arteries, pulsating with potential. The thrill tightened in my chest, synchronizing with the pulse of the city. Every whisper of fear, every murmur of speculation, every anxious glance at the news; orchestrated. Every step in the dance of panic, under my control.

I wrote one final note for the night:

“Narrative secured. Canvas five forming. Scapegoat established. Shadows watch. Art continues.”

And as Chandigarh slept, oblivious, I felt the intoxicating pulse of control. Rajiv Malhotra was a scapegoat. The public was distracted. Sebastian was suspicious but blind. And the real artist? Still free. Still alive. Still watching. Still plotting.

The game was far from over.

And I was already several moves ahead.

CHAPTER 12

Public Applause, Private Shadows

By morning, Chandigarh breathed a collective sigh of relief. Headlines plastered every newsstand, every online portal screamed the same narrative I had carefully constructed:

"Copycat Arrested! City's Fear Subsides"

"Rajiv Malhotra in Custody: Sculptor's Shadow?"

"Sculptor or Copycat? The Mystery 'Solved'?"

I sipped my espresso, pen tapping lightly against the notebook, watching the city celebrate a victory that wasn't real. Every headline, every article, every news anchor; unwitting accomplices in a story I was shaping. The thrill was subtle, like a pulse in my fingertips, and I let it flow through me, merging with the rhythm of the city itself.

Sebastian hovered nearby, a storm coiled in his posture, frown deepening with every report. "Cyra… you know this isn't over. Whoever the real killer is… they're still out there," he said quietly, voice taut with concern, dark circles under his eyes betraying restless nights.

I smiled faintly, tapping my pen against the notebook. "Yes, Sebastian. But the world sees the end. They believe it's solved. And for now… that's enough." My tone was casual, almost bored, but beneath it, the pulse of anticipation thrummed. The copycat narrative was cemented. Police, media, public; all fooled, all chasing shadows.

The first sip of espresso had grown cold, but I didn't mind. I traced the headlines again, letting the words imprint themselves. *"Fear subsides." "Mystery 'solved.'" "Sculptor's shadow captured."* Every phrase was a brick in the fortress of illusion I had built. Rajiv Malhotra, trembling journalist, scapegoat, pawn, visible face of guilt; *perfect.* The city breathed relief. I breathed control.

A thrill pulsed through me. Not from the capture itself; Rajiv had done nothing, and he knew it less than anyone; but from knowing the stage was set for the next act. The real artist remained unseen, invisible. Somewhere in the city, a shadow moved, silent and deliberate, and I could feel its pulse.

The next victim was already chosen. Someone connected. Someone high-profile. The signature would evolve. The pose would be more intricate, the roses more precise, the scene more public yet perfectly concealed. I envisioned the placement of limbs, the tilt of the head, the cascade of petals, and the exact angle from which the body would be discovered. Every detail, a statement. Every signature, a challenge to the city. And no one; not Sebastian, not the police, not the media; would suspect a thing.

Sebastian's gaze lingered on me longer than usual, sharp and calculating. "You're too calm. This… control… it's unsettling." His jaw tightened, and I could see the unspoken fear: what would happen if the real killer knew how much of the game I already understood?

I looked up, pen tapping against the edge of the desk. "Calm? No, Sebastian. I'm prepared. Thrilled, even. The thrill is in knowing the audience sees one story, while the real story… unfolds behind the curtain." My voice carried a deliberate weight, the calm of someone holding secrets others would never guess.

By mid-afternoon, I returned to Sector 14. The rain had left the streets slick, neon lights reflecting in fractured shards across puddles like broken mirrors. I walked slowly, tracing paths, imagining vantage points. The smell of damp asphalt, oil, and wet stone hung heavy in the air, mingling with the faint metallic tang that always reminded me of human blood. Every corner, every shadow, every narrow alleyway became a potential stage.

Roses would return. The pose would evolve. I imagined the victim seated or reclined in an impossible elegance, a grotesque symmetry that could only be appreciated from a singlc prccisc angle. Petals pressed against clothing, blood pooling in deliberate arcs, as if painted by a meticulous hand. Every detail would be intentional. Every element would speak a message the world was too blind to read.

The city moved around me, oblivious. Pedestrians stepped over puddles without noticing reflections of neon or the faint remnants of flower petals that might still cling to the wet asphalt. Rickshaws rattled by, tires sending droplets flying in rhythmic splashes. Somewhere a child laughed, unaware of the invisible horrors in waiting. Somewhere, a stray dog barked at nothing. Somewhere, Rajiv Malhotra cowered, believing he had been caught. Somewhere, the real killer watched, planning, refining.

I opened my notebook, pen flying across the page. Timelines, locations, connections. Each movement calculated, each exposure controlled. Public perception mapped like a chessboard: a pawn moved here, a knight distracted there, the king oblivious. Sebastian's doubts simmered silently in the corner of my mind, a reminder that even allies could be manipulated.

I reviewed the previous canvases in my mind; the businessman, the lawyer, the judge, the retired officer. Each posed with grotesque elegance, each signature evolving. The roses pressed into flesh or fabric, the subtle glyphs carved or inked onto skin, the unnatural angles, the careful staging; every act a deliberate communication. The public had seen only fragments; I had seen the entire language, and now it guided my hand.

By evening, the anticipation had become tangible. I returned to my desk at the Crime Branch, maps and sketches spread before me. Security footage, witness statements, partial prints, timelines; all integrated into a lattice of subtle misdirection. Rajiv's supposed panic anchored the story, but the true narrative was invisible. The media would applaud, the public would cheer, Sebastian would worry; all while the real killer continued unseen.

I traced my finger along the latest mapped route, imagining the perfect placement for the next scene. A penthouse balcony overlooking a crowded street? A private office with floor-to-ceiling windows, where the body would be discovered at sunrise? Every option tantalized the mind. Every choice was a challenge to the city's assumptions.

The thrill grew, sharp and electric. Control, perception, narrative; all converging. I sipped cold coffee, pen tapping a new rhythm, envisioning the next tableau. Blood, roses, precision, and the delicate balance between horror and spectacle. And in the shadows beyond the city lights, the real artist watched. Silent. Waiting. Already moving. Already composing.

Rajiv Malhotra remained behind bars, scapegoat secured. The public whispered relief, yet I could feel their unease, the residual tremors of fear. Sebastian's doubts simmered silently, a storm I had yet to provoke fully. And I… I was already steps ahead. Orchestrating. Directing. Shaping perception, guiding panic, curating fear.

The city's shadows whispered promises, and I was listening. Each alley, each corridor, each unnoticed corner became potential canvas. Each breath of the public, each glance at a headline, each whispered speculation; instruments to be played. The next act was already forming, its edges sharp, its signature unmistakable, its audience captivated yet blind.

I tapped the pen against my notebook one final time before leaning back. A single, dark thought pulsed through me:

"The audience believes. The scapegoat suffers. The real story waits. The canvas grows."

And as the city exhaled into the night, neon reflections fractured on wet streets, somewhere, the next scene was silently waiting. I was already imagining the placement of limbs, the angle of roses, the evolution of the signature. Every detail would speak a message. Only I would understand. Only I would know.

And somewhere in the darkness, the real killer smiled, unseen, thrilled by the orchestration, while I, unseen in my own right, shaped the narrative of fear, control, and anticipation.

The game was far from over. And the city, blind and trusting, danced perfectly to the rhythm I had created.

CHAPTER 13

Fractured Reflections

The city was quiet that morning, but the tension lingered like fog over Sector 9, curling through alleyways and pooling in the gaps between buildings. The memory of Judge Arvind Khanna's murder clung to the streets, to the alleys, to every neon reflection on the rain-slicked pavement. It left more than just a body; it left questions no one could answer and a shadow that stretched far beyond the crime scene itself.

I sat at my desk in the Crime Branch, pen tapping against the notebook with a rhythm that felt like a heartbeat; steady, relentless. The coffee beside me had grown cold hours ago, but I did not mind. Its bitterness seemed appropriate, matching the mood of the city and the games being played within it.

Sebastian lingered nearby, reviewing evidence, brow furrowed, hands splayed across the desk as if trying to physically restrain the chaos that hovered at the edge of comprehension.

"The fingerprints…" he muttered, voice low, almost a growl of frustration. "Partial. Inconclusive. And yet, the angles… the poses… all too precise."

I tilted my head, pen hovering over the page, letting the thought linger like smoke in a dimly lit room. "Yes, precise. Too precise, maybe. But patterns emerge from precision. The rest… the rest is interpretation."

He studied me closely, sharp eyes narrowing. "Cyra… you notice details no one else does. Sometimes too quickly. Are you sure you're… okay?"

I smiled faintly, letting the words taste bitter on my tongue. "Fine, Sebastian. Just… thinking. Overthinking, maybe. It's part of the job." My tone was casual, but inside, a thrill pulsed through me; a pulse I let simmer like heat beneath water. The thrill of patterns, of anticipation, of control.

The forensic team had uncovered something curious, something almost microscopic. Traces of rose petals clung to the judge's clothing, faintly different than the roses in the first two murders. Not scattered, but pressed subtly along the folds of his robe, as if marking his shoulders, chest, and lap with an invisible signature. The petals' edges were frayed, damp, smeared with a faint metallic scent; barely noticeable unless you knew to look.

I noted it carefully, too carefully perhaps, but that was the point. I had chosen that variation. A personal touch, evolving the signature, a way to mislead, confuse, and challenge anyone following the trail. Every detail became a cipher, and only I held the key.

Meanwhile, Rajiv Malhotra sat in custody, shivering in a small interrogation room that smelled of disinfectant and fear. Unaware he had become the city's scapegoat, he replayed every subtle nudge I had planted. Every time he had looked over his shoulder, every flinch in his interactions with journalists, every carefully "leaked" shadow captured in CCTV footage; I had orchestrated it all. The media continued to portray him as the copycat. Perfect. Every journalist who wrote a headline, every editor who ran a segment, every citizen who whispered about his guilt; oblivious to the orchestration behind the scenes.

Sebastian's unease had become a shadow between us. He hovered, not openly accusatory, but the tension in his stance betrayed a mind trying to piece together something that didn't yet exist in plain sight. He studied my notes, my gestures, my habit of tapping my pen; as if the rhythm itself might reveal a truth he couldn't yet grasp. The quiet click, click, click of graphite against paper became a metronome of controlled chaos.

Inside, a different rhythm pulsed. Thrill. Compulsion. Obsession. Patterns, signatures, narratives. I traced the timeline of murders again, imagining the next tableau with exacting detail: the tilt of a head, the angle of an arm, the way blood might drip into a pool shaped like a crescent, the placement of roses pressed like punctuation at the end of a sentence. Lighting, shadows, reflections; every detail a statement, a message, a challenge to the city that could never know the full scope.

I leaned back, cold espresso long gone, pen tracing invisible lines in the air as I mapped the streets of Chandigarh. Sector by sector, alleyway by alleyway, every reflection in wet asphalt became a potential vantage point. A passerby's glance, the rhythm of rain dripping from neon signs, the flicker of a streetlight; all became elements of staging for the next scene. The thrill of control coursed through me.

Sebastian finally broke the silence. His voice, low and uncertain, cut through the hum of the office. "Cyra… sometimes the truth is inconvenient. Sometimes the audience prefers a story that fits neatly into their fears."

I let my pen hover over the page, dark humor curling my lips. "Yes, Sebastian. Sometimes the truth is inconvenient. And sometimes… you create a version that suits the narrative."

He didn't answer. His eyes lingered longer than usual, suspicion threading through concern, doubt mingling with a reluctant respect for the speed and accuracy with which I noticed patterns. But he still didn't see. Not yet.

Outside, Chandigarh moved on, blissfully unaware. Streets glimmered with rain-soaked reflections. Buses rattled down neon-streaked streets, pedestrians hurried, umbrellas dripping. No one noticed the faint residue of rose petals along the pavement or the faint, lingering metallic scent in certain alleys. No one realized that each step, each movement of the city, played into the composition of the next scene.

I traced my finger along the map of previous victims: businessman, lawyer, judge. Each marked with a precision only I fully understood. Each spoke a language of intent, ritual, and symbolism. And now, the lines connected not just in time and space, but in narrative: a story unfolding in slow, deliberate arcs that only I could read.

I sipped the last of my cold espresso, pen tapping against the notebook again. The tapping became a cadence, each strike echoing in the room, punctuating the rhythm of anticipation. "Sebastian… the audience doesn't want the raw truth. They want a story. They want patterns they can digest, even if they're false. That's what we give them. That's what I give them."

He studied me, brow furrowed, as if he could see right through the calculated calm to the thrill beneath. "Cyra… you're not just observing anymore. You're shaping this. You're… guiding it. It's dangerous."

I smiled faintly, letting the edge of dark humor linger in my words. "Dangerous is subjective. Thrilling, maybe. Artful, definitely. Control is the key. And control is mine."

The forensic updates trickled in. Partial prints, smudged glyphs carved into surfaces, droplets of blood that hinted at life, yet preserved nothing that could identify the real artist; all meticulously staged. Every piece of evidence fit perfectly within the narrative I was constructing. Rajiv Malhotra's supposed panic, his frantic explanations, the leaks I'd orchestrated; all perfectly aligned with the false trail I wanted the city to follow.

Sebastian glanced at me, unease and admiration warring across his face. "Cyra… you've never seen patterns like this before. Or maybe… you've always seen them." His voice trembled slightly, betraying the tension he tried to mask.

I tapped my pen against the edge of the notebook, letting the sound echo in the otherwise quiet office. "Patterns exist everywhere, Sebastian. You just have to know where to look. And sometimes… you have to create them yourself."

His jaw clenched, and for a moment, I could see the storm behind his eyes. Concern, fear, suspicion; tangled together, but never fully forming into accusation. Good. Let him stew. Let him question himself before he questions me.

The city outside continued its oblivious routine. Neon reflections shimmered in puddles, car horns honked in rhythmic patterns, and the faint smell of wet asphalt and rain-dampened concrete hung heavy in the air. Somewhere, the next victim moved unknowingly, a piece in a narrative already written but unseen. Somewhere, the killer prepared, unseen, precise, patient.

I traced the lines between victims once more, imagining the next tableau in agonizing detail. Perhaps the next would be a woman; influential, untouchable, poised in a room full of light and shadows, the roses pressed with intent, the body arranged as if frozen mid-thought, mid-gesture. The petals would carry a faint metallic tang, edges frayed to perfection. Blood would pool along lines calculated to evoke unease, the lighting casting deliberate reflections. Only the right observer would see the message.

The thrill of anticipation pulsed stronger now, almost electric. The control, the orchestration, the careful manipulation of perception; every element of the city, every pulse of its citizens, every headline, every whisper, every shadowed glance; all a part of a performance. A symphony of fear, order, and illusion. And I was the conductor.

I leaned back, dark thoughts curling like smoke around me. The previous victims; businessman, lawyer, judge, retired officer; all part of a narrative, but incomplete without the next act. And I could see it forming: angles, lighting, reflections, the careful placement of roses and subtle glyphs. Every detail, a punctuation in the ongoing story, every choice deliberate, every act a testament to control.

Rajiv remained the city's scapegoat, whispered about in the news, analyzed by commentators, feared by the public; yet completely oblivious to the manipulation. Sebastian's doubts lingered, shadowed and sharp, but he still could not see the full picture. And I…

I was already several steps ahead, orchestrating the next act, predicting reactions, curating horror, staging fear, and delighting in the invisible strings I held.

Outside, Chandigarh breathed, unaware of the careful choreography behind every shadow, every puddle, every reflection in wet asphalt. Somewhere in the city, the next tableau waited. Somewhere, roses would press against flesh or fabric in deliberate arcs, blood would trace silent punctuation, and the world would see only fragments of the truth.

And I… was ready.

CHAPTER 14

Pressure Points

Rajiv Malhotra had begun to unravel. The subtle nudges I had planted were no longer whispers in the dark. They were pounding drums in his mind, each one echoing louder than the last. A shadow in a hallway that wasn't really there, a misremembered detail from an interview, a fleeting figure glimpsed through half-lit windows; I ensured each tiny fragment reached him.

Anonymous tips, “accidental” leaks to journalists, blurred security footage; all orchestrated, all deliberate. The perfect pressure points. Every subtle push made him twitch, sweat, and second-guess.

I sat at my desk in the Crime Branch, pen tapping rhythmically against thc leather-bound notebook, a metronome marking the pulse of controlled chaos. Each strike was deliberate, each tap a reminder of the patterns I had constructed, the paths I had aligned. Sebastian leaned against the wall, arms crossed, eyes narrowing, every muscle tense. He had begun to sense the magnitude of what I was doing.

“Cyra… he’s cracking,” he muttered, voice low, tight with tension. “We might be pushing him too far.”

I smiled faintly, letting the faintest curl of dark humor touch my lips. “Good. Fear is clarifying. People reveal themselves under pressure.” My words sounded casual, but beneath the surface, there was a thrill that coiled tighter with each beat of my heart. The thrill of watching the narrative bend, shift, and unravel at my fingertips.

Rajiv’s interviews became public spectacles. Each response, more nervous than the last. Each gesture twitchier, as though his limbs themselves had been wired to a confession that didn’t exist. Every misstep, a breadcrumb I left for the media, the police, and the city to interpret as guilt. Every stuttered word, every flinch, every glimmer of uncertainty; all tools I wielded invisibly.

And yet something inside me stirred differently that day. A flicker I did not fully recognize. Sleep deprivation? Obsession sharpened by weeks of careful manipulation? Perhaps a hint of thrill too close to the edge? My hands shook slightly as I took notes, pen scratching across the page, tracing imagined angles, plotting trajectories of bodies yet to exist. Sebastian's glance caught mine. His suspicion had grown sharper, honed into a blade I could feel pressing against my conscience, though I did not flinch.

Later, while reviewing timelines of the past three murders, I traced trajectories, poses, and signatures. My pen hovered over subtle variations; rose petals slightly rearranged, angles shifted, precision adjusted; small, almost imperceptible details that only I could notice. Only I could orchestrate. Each line drawn on the notebook was a prelude, each connection mapped a step toward the inevitable next canvas. The thrill of anticipation was almost tangible, a pulse racing beneath my skin.

Sebastian approached quietly, the leather of his shoes soft against the linoleum floor. "Cyra… you've been tapping that pen nonstop. It's distracting. Are you… okay?"

I let the dark humor curl at the edges of my lips. "Old man, pens talk. They tell stories. And I listen."

The words hung between us, deceptively light, but I could see the tightening in his jaw, the unspoken warning in his eyes. He didn't trust the calm I displayed. He could feel, perhaps, the undercurrent of compulsion that guided my actions.

He frowned, the concern and suspicion mingling in his gaze. "Cyra… the next one… you feel it coming, don't you?"

I paused, pen hovering, mid-air, the tiny circle of graphite suspended above the page like a question mark I could not answer.

"Maybe I do. Maybe I've been waiting."

The words felt heavier than I intended, imbued with a gravity that even I could not entirely contain. I tapped the pen again, forcing control back into the rhythm, letting the motion anchor me to the present.

Outside, Chandigarh moved on, oblivious. The streets shimmered with reflections from puddles and neon signs, the faint smell of wet asphalt lingering in the air. The city slept, commuters rushed, streetlights flickered, and the world celebrated a narrative that was carefully, almost cruelly, misaligned. Headlines escalated Rajiv's fear into certainty: the copycat had been identified. The public cheered a victory that wasn't real. Perfect.

Inside, a different pulse ran beneath the surface. Something darker, something urgent. A craving for the next canvas, the next stage, the next body carefully arranged and meticulously framed. The thrill of anticipation coursed through me, heating my veins, sharpening my senses. I could almost feel it; the tactile thrill of arranging petals, the metallic tang of blood in the air, the precise angles that made a tableau speak a language only I fully understood.

I imagined the next scene. The victim would be high-profile. The pose, deliberate. Perhaps a young politician, someone untouchable in the public eye, seated as though frozen mid-speech, a microphone at an impossible angle, roses pressed into the folds of a crisp suit, petals dampened with rain and blood. I traced the scene in my mind, imagining how light would fall across the face, casting shadows across a cheekbone, outlining the tilt of a head. Each droplet of red a punctuation, each shadow a sentence in a language of horror and control.

Sebastian's presence lingered at my shoulder like a specter, silent but palpable. I could feel the tension coil between us, unspoken and thick. "Cyra…" he began, voice soft, cautious. "Do you ever stop? Planning, orchestrating… this… game?"

I looked at him, pen tapping once, twice, three times against the notebook. "Stop?" I whispered, voice low, almost a conspiratorial hum. "Why would I stop? The game has just begun. The audience believes they're following the story, but the truth… the truth is mine."

His eyes narrowed, a mix of fear and fascination swimming in their depths. He could sense the obsession that had begun to consume me. He could sense the compulsion, the hunger for the next act, the way my mind traced trajectories not just of bodies, but of perception itself. He did not yet know the extent. And perhaps, it was better that he did not.

I revisited every timeline, every image, every note. Each murder traced a line across the city, connecting the powerful, the untouchable, the corrupt. The judge, the lawyer, the businessman, the retired officer; each selection deliberate, each tableau carefully composed. And now, the anticipation of the next act; richer, more personal, more public; consumed me. The thrill of creation, of control, of invisibly conducting the city's fear, pulsed stronger than ever.

In the quiet of my office, I let the thought linger. The next victim would not simply be another in a series. They would be a statement. A reflection of power, of influence, of corruption. And they would be arranged to be understood; only by those who looked closely enough. By those who could see beyond the surface. By me.

The rose petals. Always the roses. Their scent, metallic and sweet, would linger in the air. Their placement, precise. Their meaning, hidden yet deliberate. And blood, subtle, perfectly staged to speak without shouting, to suggest without revealing.

I traced my finger across the map once more, imagining the angles, the reflections, the trajectories. Each alleyway, each window, each neon reflection became part of the composition. The city itself was a gallery. Every passerby, an unwitting observer. Every journalist, a curator of a false story. Every citizen, an audience to a play staged from shadows.

Rajiv Malhotra remained unaware of the full scope. The public believed him to be the copycat, their scapegoat. The media continued to amplify his supposed guilt. Sebastian remained on the precipice of understanding, suspicion warring with disbelief. And I… I was already steps ahead, orchestrating not just the next tableau, but the city's perception of it, the thrill of anticipation, the compulsion to create, the craving for the next canvas.

Outside, Chandigarh slept beneath a sky streaked with fading rain clouds, neon reflections rippling in puddles. Somewhere, the next victim moved unknowingly, an actor in a story already written, framed for a narrative they could not yet see. Somewhere, the roses waited, the petals damp, the arrangement precise, the tableau prepared.

And I… was ready.

CHAPTER 15

Close to the Edge

The call came just past midnight. Another body. Sector 19, on the outskirts of Chandigarh's industrial belt. The streets smelled of wet asphalt, diesel, and the faint smoke from factories still burning through the night. The city seemed muted under the low clouds, the usual hum of traffic replaced by the whisper of rain dripping from rooftops.

I drove through the dark, Sebastian beside me, quiet and tense. The neon glow of distant signs fractured across the wet pavement, reflected in puddles like shards of colored glass. The distorted reflections seemed alive, twisting and stretching with each turn, each curve of the road. The city looked beautiful in its own way, sinister and fractured, a mirror to what awaited.

The victim was a senior officer in the city's crime department, a man whose reputation for cracking corruption had earned him respect and enemies in equal measure. His body had been positioned with ceremonial precision. Hands folded over his chest, head tilted slightly, eyes wide and staring into a void. Red roses lay beside him, petals wet, some smudged with crimson. The signature was intact. The evolution of the killer's work was clear.

I crouched beside him, notebook in hand. Coffee long cold on the dashboard, pen poised to capture every detail. Each victim was a statement, each scene a message. Calculated. Meticulous. The thrill of recognition pulsed through me. This was artistry. Horror intertwined with discipline, chaos framed like a painting.

Sebastian's voice cut quietly through the night. "Cyra, the killer is escalating. This is no longer just about sending a message. This is personal. The proximity… it is too close."

I nodded, tapping my pen lightly against the notebook cover. "Patterns evolve, Sebastian. The message adapts. The killer knows the city, the people, the routines."

A flicker of unease ran through me. Small details unsettled me. A footprint slightly off to the side, a rose petal misplaced on the polished floor. Minor imperfections, almost imperceptible, but enough to prick at my certainty. My hands shook slightly as I recorded them. Fatigue? Obsession? A slip? Only I would ever know. Every note I took was a combination of observation and projection, a ritual of control over what might soon be chaos.

Back at the Crime Branch, I mapped the timeline, the sequence of events. Sebastian lingered closer now, watching my methods, my focus, my pen movements. His eyes were sharp, a mixture of concern and growing suspicion. "Cyra, sometimes you see too clearly. Or maybe you see what you want to see."

I allowed a faint smile, dark humor curling around the edges of my lips. Tapping my pen against the edge of the desk, I said, "Perception is subjective. The world believes what it wants. And we guide them without them realizing it." My voice was calm, but inside, the pulse of anticipation had accelerated.

As I traced the trajectory of the victims, the thrill pulsed differently this time. Sharper. Darker. Closer to obsession. The canvas was no longer just a series of statements. It was expanding, folding inward, touching nerves and lines I had not yet crossed. Every calculation was a test, every observation a rehearsal for something bigger. The stakes were higher. The line between watching and participating was beginning to blur.

The details of the scene replayed in my mind. The angle of the officer's head. The tilt of his fingers. The placement of the roses. The way the shadows from overhead lights fell across the polished floor, slicing the room into sharp rectangles. Every element had meaning, if one knew how to read it. The small imperfections; a dropped petal, a smear of blood too faint to alarm; were deliberate whispers to anyone paying attention, though no one ever would.

Outside, Chandigarh slept under a sky blurred by rain and neon reflections. Puddles shimmered like black glass, distorting the occasional passerby into ghostly shapes. The city had no idea that the artist they feared, admired, and hunted had been standing in plain sight all along. The hunt, the fear, the anticipation; all part of the performance I was orchestrating.

Sebastian's presence remained tangible, almost a shadow in the corner of my mind. He was close, yet not close enough to touch the truth. He sensed something shifting, a subtle tension between order and compulsion, control and obsession. But he could not see the full picture. He did not yet understand that the canvas was not only expanding across the city but reaching inward, into me.

I allowed myself a moment to breathe, pen hovering over the notebook, imagining the next stage. The next victim would not be merely another name on a list. They would be someone high-profile, someone untouchable. The tableau would evolve, becoming more intricate. Roses would return, but their arrangement would carry nuance. Each petal, each angle, each droplet of blood would be deliberate, a cipher meant to communicate beyond what the public could comprehend.

The thrill of creation was intoxicating. The control over perception, over fear, over panic; it pulsed through me with every breath. The city's streets, slick and deserted, reflected the potential of what was to come. Every corner, every alley, every reflective puddle became a part of the design. Chandigarh itself was an unwitting gallery for the next tableau.

I imagined the scene in meticulous detail. The victim seated, posed mid-action, perhaps frozen mid-conversation, microphone tilted, hand gestures arrested mid-motion. Red roses carefully tucked into creases of clothing. Petals dampened with rain and subtle traces of crimson. Shadows from distant neon and overhead lights would form patterns, almost like commentary, like punctuation to a silent story. The final image would be impossible to ignore and impossible to interpret fully. Only I would know its meaning.

Sebastian's voice broke my contemplation. "Cyra, how do you keep this level of focus? How do you keep orchestrating everything without… slipping?"

I met his gaze, letting my eyes glint. "Slipping requires surrender. Control requires attention. The audience never notices the hand guiding the narrative." I tapped my pen lightly, the rhythm steady and deliberate. "We shape perception without anyone realizing. That is the art."

He studied me, unease settling like a stone in his chest. Suspicion warred with disbelief. He could feel the undercurrent of obsession but could not name it. He would never see the full picture until it was already completed.

I returned to my notebook, mapping trajectories, timelines, and positions. I traced the movements of each victim through the city, each tableau connecting like threads in an invisible tapestry. Each minor variation, each intentional imperfection, added complexity. Every detail mattered. Every subtlety whispered a story to those who knew how to read it.

Outside, the city remained unaware, sleeping beneath neon lights, puddles shimmering with distorted reflections. Somewhere, the next victim moved, oblivious to the fact that they had already been written into the canvas of fear and precision. Somewhere, the roses waited, the petals damp, arranged in anticipation of a statement yet to be made.

And I, perched above the narrative, the orchestrator of fear and fascination, was already planning the next tableau. Every detail, every nuance, every stroke of imagination had a purpose. The line between observation and obsession had blurred entirely. The thrill of creation pulsed stronger than ever.

Chandigarh did not yet know that the artist they sought had been present all along, manipulating perception, guiding fear, and weaving a story that was far larger, far darker, than anyone could imagine.

I closed my notebook, tapping the pen once more. Outside, the night was quiet, deceptive in its calm. But within the chaos I had set in motion, the next masterpiece was already forming. Every shadow, every reflection, every heartbeat in the city would become part of it.

And I… was ready.

CHAPTER 16

The Mirror Case

The city woke to headlines screaming about the murder in Sector 19. Every newspaper screamed the same story, bold letters designed to instill fear:

"KILLER STRIKES AGAIN: IS THE COPYCAT STILL AT LARGE?"

Beneath the letters, Rajiv Malhotra's mugshot stared back from every newsstand, a contradiction wrapped in media frenzy. He was already in custody. The world wanted answers, demanded closure, craved a villain it could see and name. The truth was far more complicated, hidden beneath layers only I could navigate.

At the Crime Branch, I stood over the evidence board, red thread stretching across photographs, timelines, maps, and notes. Each line traced a path between victims, between moments, connecting shadows and reflections, whispers and screams. My pen tapped in sync with my thoughts, a metronome to keep the chaos orderly. Coffee stains dotted the edges of my papers, smudges of exhaustion and caffeine.

I drew another line. Too straight, too knowing. The trajectory from victim one to victim four formed more than a pattern. It was a map of choices I had made quietly, in silence. Each decision etched across time and space, perfectly aligned yet invisible to everyone else.

For a moment, I froze. The handwriting on the page felt unfamiliar. As if someone else had drawn it. As if another mind had slipped into mine and guided the line across the board. It was a sensation that prickled my skin, something I could not place. It was thrilling and terrifying all at once. My own thoughts, so carefully curated, felt borrowed.

Sebastian entered quietly, file in hand, his presence deliberate, almost intrusive. He placed it on the desk without a word. I glanced down at the photographs inside. Close-ups of petals, the precise positioning of bodies, the angles of limbs. Each shot dissected the scenes in a way that made the arrangements almost clinical, almost sacred.

He had marked inconsistencies in my notes, small variations, subtle shifts, details I had overlooked—or perhaps ignored.

"Your deductions," he said carefully, voice low, cautious, "they are too precise. Almost as if you knew what you would find before you found it."

I forced a laugh, sharp, bitter, tasting of fear I refused to admit aloud. "Experience, Sebastian. Sometimes instinct masquerades as foresight." My pen continued to tap against the edge of the table, but my hands shook beneath the rhythm.

Later, during the autopsy briefing, I noticed something that no one else did. A faint mark on the victim's wrist, a pale abrasion like a rope burn. The forensic officer had not mentioned it, not even in passing. I interrupted, my voice calm, measured, precise.

"Look here," I said, pointing at the photograph, tracing the faint line with a gloved finger. "See the mark on the wrist? It suggests restraint before death. Timing. Positioning. The killer was deliberate."

Several officers exchanged impressed looks. Sebastian did not. He watched me, his eyes narrowing, a combination of paternal concern and growing doubt. His silence was heavier than approval.

After the briefing, he pulled me aside into the empty hallway. The Crime Branch felt unusually quiet, the hum of fluorescent lights filling the space with an oppressive white glow.

“Cyra,” he said, voice low, almost urgent. “You are working yourself to the point of exhaustion. You cannot keep living off coffee and instinct. You need rest. You are pushing yourself beyond reason.”

I stared at him, pen tapping against my thigh, a slow, deliberate rhythm. “Rest is for the innocent,” I said quietly. There was no room for rest in this game, no room for pause. Every moment unattended could mean a detail missed, a line untraced, a pattern incomplete.

He sighed, his hand lingering on my shoulder longer than necessary. His touch carried the weight of suspicion, of worry, of something unspoken. A tension that neither of us could name. I did not flinch. Not outwardly. Inside, a shadow of unease crawled along my spine.

That night, alone in my apartment, I replayed the patterns over and over in my mind. The roses, the meticulous arrangements, the faint variations. Each victim’s pose had been rehearsed in imagination, each scene a test of my ability to control narrative, perception, and reaction. I traced every trajectory with invisible fingers, repositioned petals, re-angled limbs in my mind.

I sat in front of the mirror, pen still tapping against the notebook. My reflection stared back at me. Hollow eyes. Skin pale from exhaustion. Lips pressed in concentration. For a split second, I did not recognize the person staring back. My own reflection had become unfamiliar, as if the obsession that guided my actions had also stolen my identity.

The reflection in the mirror was sharp, cruel, almost accusatory. Every shadow beneath the eyes whispered truths I refused to admit. I realized, suddenly, that the meticulous control I exerted over the city, the media, the investigation, and even the copycat suspect, had exacted a cost I could not measure. It was not just the others who were being manipulated. I was also a prisoner of my own game.

Images of the latest scene flickered in my mind. The victim seated in the chair, the roses arranged with deliberate imperfection, the slight smear of crimson that caught the light just enough to be noticed but not enough to alarm. I had orchestrated chaos while the world looked for order. And yet now, staring at myself, the line between orchestrator and participant blurred entirely.

Sebastian's words echoed through the apartment: "You cannot keep living off instinct alone." They were not merely warnings. They were mirrors. A reflection of my own edge, the thin line between precision and obsession, control and surrender.

I looked again at the mirror. The eyes staring back blinked slowly, deliberately. I knew them. I knew myself. And I did not. It was the paradox of the work, the thrill, the compulsion that had drawn me this far. The thrill of seeing the city react, of watching fear propagate, of shaping panic into narrative. Yet there, in the quiet, in the reflection, I saw another truth.

A possibility. That my obsession, my control, my very intuition, was becoming indistinguishable from the killer's hand. That the patterns I traced, the signatures I followed, might not just reflect the city's murderer. They might also reflect me.

I closed the notebook slowly, pen resting atop it. The tapping had stopped, replaced by a quieter pulse. The pulse of anticipation, of inevitability. The next victim, the next tableau, the next variation; it was forming even as I stared at my reflection. My reflection, tired and hollow, understood the inevitability before I fully did.

Sleep would not come. Rest was a luxury the innocent might afford. I was no longer innocent. The copycat was contained, the scapegoat in place, yet the real story was unfolding in a direction only I could trace. And as I stared at my own eyes, I realized the truth that had been whispering to me all along: the canvas of terror was no longer just the city. The canvas included me.

I left the mirror, walked to the window, and gazed over the neon reflections in puddles and rain-slick streets. Somewhere, someone slept, unaware of the unseen hands shaping their perception. Somewhere, the next masterpiece waited. And somewhere, I had to face the reflection that had begun to move independently, that had begun to challenge even me.

And I was not afraid.

Not yet.

The mirror had shown me the edge. The city had shown me the patterns. And now, only I could navigate the space between control and obsession, between shadow and self. The game had not ended. It had only begun to look back.

CHAPTER 17

Parallel Lines

Sebastian had always been steady. A constant in the chaos. The gravelly voice that kept me anchored when the storm of the city threatened to sweep me off balance. He had always been predictable. Reliable. Calm. But lately, something had shifted. That voice, once grounding, carried a weight I could not place. Not anger. Not disappointment. Something heavier.

Doubt.

At the Crime Branch, his presence had changed subtly. He asked fewer questions in public, his tone measured, almost cautious. Yet he lingered longer after meetings, eyes tracing my notes, following the rhythm of my pen as it tapped against the table like a metronome counting down seconds to inevitability. I could feel it, a quiet tension threading through the room whenever he was near, a pressure that tugged at my instincts.

By evening, I noticed something unusual. Sebastian had left before me. Always the last to leave. He never skipped the rhythm of the night, never left the evidence board unattended. I filed it away at first as fatigue or distraction. But the next day, I learned the truth.

Two nights later, I saw him near Sector 26 grain market. A location that bore no connection to any of our current leads. He wasn't meeting informants. He wasn't conducting field checks. He was speaking quietly with officers from the Forensics Bureau. I kept my distance, observing him as a careful shadow. His back was straight, posture stiff, hands gesturing occasionally. They were not casual gestures. He was deliberate, meticulous. The kind of movement that spoke of someone tracing lines, connecting dots.

When he returned to the Branch the next morning, he did not mention it. He acted as though nothing had shifted. But the subtle differences were impossible to ignore. Files were kept closer, notes double-checked, questions phrased with caution. His silences had lengthened. He moved through the office like a shadow in the corner of a room; present, but calculating, considering. Watching.

Then came the request that set my mind alight with both thrill and apprehension.

"Cyra," he said quietly, voice calm but deliberate, "I need your case notes from the first murder. Handwritten, not the copies."

I arched an eyebrow. "Why? You already have them."

"I want to compare your initial impressions with where we are now. Fresh eyes."

I laughed, a bitter twist at the corners of my lips. "Fresh eyes or suspicious ones?"

He did not laugh back. His gaze was steady, unwavering, almost piercing. I felt the stirrings of unease as his eyes met mine, as if he could look past the words and into the spaces between them. Into me.

Inside, something churned. Not fear. Not exactly. A flicker of thrill. A flicker of danger. Questions began to spin. Was he piecing it together? Could he? The thought sent an electric pulse through my veins, a mixture of anticipation and caution, thrill and compulsion.

Later that night, I walked through Sector 22. Neon lights glowed against rain-slick streets, their reflections fractured and elongated across puddles, fractured like the fragments of a mind at work. The city hummed with life. Horns honked, distant voices laughed, shadows moved across walls and alleys. All of it was vivid, alive, and yet my attention rested on the narrative I was weaving.

The roses were ready. Petals glistening with the memory of rain, the scent faint but unmistakable. The tools were sharpened. Instruments of precision, of control. Every detail chosen, measured, rehearsed in my mind. The story demanded its next chapter. And I would provide it.

But Sebastian had changed the equation. My anchor, my father figure, the one I trusted to be steady, was no longer just watching over me. He had stepped out of the background and into observation. He was not merely supervising the case. He was watching me. The way a predator studies movement without making a sound. The way a chess player studies a board, not to play, but to anticipate.

I felt the shift in the air, in the rhythm of my thoughts, in the tapping of my pen. A new tension had entered the room, the city, and my mind. Every decision, every choice, every movement carried weight beyond the immediate canvas of murder and pattern. Sebastian's scrutiny became another variable in the game. Another line that ran parallel to my own, not intersecting yet, but impossibly close.

And the thrill, the compulsion that had driven me this far, pulsed sharper now. Not from the murders. Not from the city. But from the knowledge that someone I trusted could see me, analyze me, trace the hidden lines of thought I had always believed were mine alone.

The next canvas would be different. The stakes had escalated. The pattern had shifted. And I had to be both the artist and the observer of my own work. Every step, every petal, every scene now carried a new significance. Sebastian's presence was no longer a comfort. It was a challenge. A question written in the subtle lines of his expression, the pauses in his words, the weight of his gaze.

I walked further down the street, neon reflections streaking across wet asphalt, and allowed the thought to settle in the edges of my mind. The game was no longer solely about control of the city, of perception, or of narrative. It was now about parallel lines; my actions, my obsessions, and the eyes that were tracing them alongside me. Lines that moved in the same space, close enough to collide, close enough to alter trajectories.

I smiled faintly to myself, tapping my pen against the notebook I carried in my coat pocket. The thrill of creation had always been intoxicating. The thrill of observation had always been a craving. Now, the thrill of challenge had entered. Sebastian had become another factor in the unfolding design.

The roses awaited. The story demanded continuation. The tools were sharpened, and my mind was alive with the possibilities of the next tableau. The city slept unaware, yet its shadows whispered of anticipation.

And I moved through the streets, silent and deliberate, knowing that someone; someone I trusted; was no longer just a companion in this storm. He was a parallel line, close, precise, and impossibly aligned. Watching. Waiting. Calculating.

And I… I was already planning the next move.

CHAPTER 18

The Unintended Mark

The compulsion arrived like hunger — sharp, insistent, impossible to ignore. It gnawed at my chest, at my hands, at the rhythm of my thoughts. I told myself it was the investigation, the puzzle, the chase. But deep inside, I knew better.

I haven't been completely honest with you. It's time we see reality, not the narrative.

The roses were already in my bag. The gloves tucked neatly in the pocket of my coat. My hands trembled until I gave them purpose.

It had to happen again.

The target was clear: Ramesh Tandon, a property dealer infamous for bribery and land scams. A man who had slipped through the legal cracks of Chandigarh for years. A man who deserved attention, attention delivered in silence, meticulously crafted. The perfect canvas.

I waited near Sector 17 Plaza, blending into the throng of neon lights and loud music spilling from bars. He staggered from one such bar, jacket half-open, tie askew, swaying against the crowd's pulse. No one noticed me as I shadowed him, footsteps light, gloved hands ready.

The alley behind the shopping complex offered privacy. Dim, narrow, lined with dumpsters and slick brick. I followed him inside, my heartbeat syncing with the drip of rainwater from the corrugated roof above.

It was quick. Efficient. Practiced. My hands stopped trembling only when his body slumped against the cold wall, an inert form in the wet darkness.

I posed him carefully; hands folded, a rose nestled in his lapel, eyes open to the sky as if pleading for understanding. Every fold of fabric, every angle of a limb, deliberate. Signature intact. Precision maintained.

But something slipped.

The rain had returned unexpectedly, a cold wash that streaked down the alley. My movement was slightly rushed. The rose petals clung to my glove, tearing. A fragment of one stubborn petal adhered to the seam of my coat sleeve. I didn't notice at the time, absorbed in the rhythm of creation, the silent choreography of order imposed on chaos.

Later, at the Crime Branch, Sebastian studied the photographs of the scene with unusual intensity. "Curious," he murmured, pointing to a faint smudge on the brick wall. "Almost like… a handprint, but blurred. The angles don't align with the suspect we've profiled."

I forced a laugh, tapping my pen against the desk harder than usual. "Rain distorts everything. You're chasing ghosts."

But his eyes lingered on me longer than on the photograph, tracking the movement, the hesitation, the posture. His gaze wasn't casual. It was calibrated, precise, unrelenting.

Hours later, as I rewrote my notes in the dim light of my office, my attention flicked to my coat draped over the chair. There it was; the torn petal, half-hidden in the seam. My chest tightened. My pulse surged. My hands trembled again, the rhythm I had mastered slipping like sand through fingers.

A knock at the office door broke my focus. Calm, casual. Controlled.

"Coffee?" Sebastian's voice was steady, but there was an undercurrent I could feel. Not accusation. Not yet. Observation.

I nodded, forcing a smile. "Always."

He stepped inside, eyes flicking to the coat, then to the desk, to my notebook, to the faintly trembling pen in my hand. He did not comment. He did not move hastily. But the air between us shifted, taut, loaded with tension.

Something had cracked inside me. I had left a trace. One tiny, overlooked fragment. And Sebastian — patient, calculating Sebastian — would not let it go unnoticed.

I returned to my notes, pen tapping lightly, pretending rhythm, pretending calm. But beneath it all, a quiet alarm pulsed. One fragment, one oversight, one unintended mark. It was a crack in perfection, a slip in control.

And I knew he had seen it.

The next step would require focus, precision, and an even sharper awareness of my own movements. One mistake was tolerable. Two would be dangerous.

The roses in my bag, damp and fragrant, were a reminder that creation had no room for error. The city waited for the narrative to unfold. The public, Rajiv, Sebastian; none of them had any idea what had truly happened.

But the unintended mark was now part of the equation.

And I would have to account for it.

CHAPTER 19

Under Watch

Sebastian had grown quieter. Not absent, not cold — just measured. Every question he asked was carefully worded, every glance held a fraction too long. He moved through the Crime Branch with the calm precision of a man who had always been one step ahead, but now his attention seemed directed squarely at me.

At the Branch, he requested full access to the forensic archives, citing "cross-case comparisons." No one questioned him; he carried respect like armor, almost legendary. But I watched him from the corner of my eye as he sifted through photographs, fingerprints, fiber reports. Each movement deliberate. Each pause loaded. His silence carried weight. It demanded answers without asking for them.

One evening, I caught him studying the blurred handprint from the last crime scene, magnified on his laptop. He traced its angles, carefully, against a database of known prints. Slowly. Patiently. Every finger, every arc scrutinized.

When he noticed me at the doorway, he closed the file. Too quickly.

"Working late?" I asked lightly, pen tapping against the frame.

He offered the faintest smile. "Always."

But the tone had shifted; not mentor to student, not father to daughter. Investigator to suspect.

I felt the shift immediately. The thrill of control now came with a tremor. The hunter I had played with for so long might be hunting me.

To counter, I doubled down.

I leaked a tip to a journalist at Sector 34 Press Colony, a whisper that Rajiv Malhotra had bribed someone inside the jail for outside help. Within hours, headlines screamed again: *"Copycat Killer Still Active Despite Arrest!"*

I suggested in meetings that Rajiv had accomplices — younger men, desperate, eager to imitate his style. I even dragged in the name of an old rival detective, weaving just enough plausible detail to cloud the waters.

The Branch followed my lead, as they always did. Perfect execution. The admired cynic with a nose for patterns, untouchable in public eyes.

But Sebastian did not follow.

That night, as we walked from the office, his steps were measured, deliberate, slower than mine. The drizzle slicked pavement reflected Sector 17's neon lights, fractured in puddles. He spoke, voice low, deliberate, carrying weight I could not ignore.

"You've built a convincing case against Rajiv, Cyra. Too convincing. Almost like… someone wanted it that way."

My pen froze mid-tap. "Are you accusing me, Sebastian?"

His gaze held mine, steady, heavy with something unsaid. "I'm asking you to be careful. Obsession blinds good detectives. Even the best."

We stood there in the rain, the city alive around us, oblivious to the quiet war unfolding. The hum of engines, the chatter of pedestrians, the neon flicker; all drowned beneath the tension between us.

I understood, in that moment, the true shift. He was no longer just suspicious. He was collecting evidence, piecing it together, testing patterns against behavior. Piece by piece, thread by thread.

The noose was tightening.

And I, who had always orchestrated the story, realized I might now be part of someone else's narrative.

CHAPTER 20

Shadows in the Rain

The night was alive with the sound of rain. Not the soft drizzle that glided over the city in the early evening, but the hard, insistent kind that turned streets into mirrors. Sector 15 glimmered in neon reflections, the puddles catching every red, green, and yellow light, distorting them like shattered glass. I drove through it all, hands gripping the wheel, the compulsion thrumming in my veins, louder than the wipers, sharper than the smell of wet asphalt.

Sebastian's headlights appeared in the rearview mirror before I consciously registered them. Too steady, too familiar. Watching. Testing. Patient.

For a moment, I allowed myself to imagine abandoning everything; the car, the streetlights, the city's judgment; and stepping into the darkness. Another canvas. Another tableau. But he was there. Close enough to see. Close enough to prevent me. Close enough to know.

I turned sharply into the lanes of Sector 22, weaving past shuttered shops and sleeping houses. Neon signs flickered and reflected in puddles, fragments of light broken across uneven asphalt. The compulsion was constant, insistent, but the knowledge of him, quiet yet omnipresent, added an edge to it. Fear? Maybe. But not fear in the way an innocent might feel it. Fear as in an adversary recognizing your rhythm before you've even begun.

I parked near Shanti Kunj Garden, the car tires hissing in the shallow water. Pretending to light a cigarette, I didn't. The gesture was enough; smoke imaginary, a performance in front of my own reflection. My hands brushed against the bag on the passenger seat. Inside, the roses rested, their petals damp and fragrant. My fingers itched to reach in, to arrange, to place. The compulsion beat like a second heartbeat.

Minutes passed. I counted them silently. Each tick of my pen against the steering wheel louder than the rain. Every reflection in the glass around me was fractured; streetlights, neon signs, puddles, my own eyes. Hollow-eyed. Lips curling in a smile that felt borrowed from someone else, someone I didn't entirely recognize.

Sebastian's presence was not overt. His car idled across the street, far enough to blend into shadows but close enough to remind me he was watching. He wasn't questioning me. He wasn't talking. He simply existed as a constant, measuring force; the anchor I had relied on, now an unseen opponent in a game I had thought I controlled.

I imagined his thoughts. Patient. Calculating. Observing. Piecing together the puzzle of me while I played the predator. And for a second, my heart raced in a way the murders never made it race. Not excitement, not compulsion; calculation. Anticipation. Recognition.

I drove slowly along the narrow lanes, turning left and right, circling the garden, tracing the curves of the streets, each movement deliberate. The rain had dulled the scent of exhaust, masked the subtle scrape of tires against worn asphalt. Perfect cover for those who walked unseen, those who watched, those who waited.

The compulsion tightened its grip, and I imagined Ramesh Tandon, the man I made the next canvas. His stagger from the bar, jacket slung, tie loose. The alley behind the shopping complex, neon flickered above his head. The precision in which his body fell into place, the folded hands, the rose at his chest, eyes wide to the night sky. All of it in my head. Perfect.

I wanted it more. I wanted to move, to act. But Sebastian's headlights pressed against my consciousness like a reminder of boundaries, like a tether holding me back. A test. He was watching to see if I would break. To see if I would give in to instinct over prudence.

I parked the car at the edge of the garden and let my body relax slightly, hands still on the wheel. I could feel the warmth of the steering wheel through the gloves. My breathing synced with the patter of rain, the distant honk of a horn, the occasional shout from someone closing a shop. Time slowed, the world condensed into the space between me and him, the space between wanting and restraint.

The city was unaware. It never saw the subtle, careful movements of those who shaped its narratives. The neon flickers reflected in puddles, shadows pooling at corners, whispered promises from darkness. And I was listening. Always listening. Waiting.

Minutes dragged, each second stretching into a canvas of tension. My reflection stared back at me; pale skin, dark eyes, pen in hand, lips curled. Hollow, focused. The reflection almost didn't feel like me. And perhaps it wasn't. Perhaps it was the part of me that existed only when the city was quiet, when rain was loud, when no one was looking. The part that planned. The part that executed. The part that craved the control I wielded so effortlessly over the chaos of others.

Finally, I started the engine. Smooth. Silent. Controlled. Turning toward Madhya Marg, tracing paths familiar to Sebastian, letting him follow. The rearview mirror reflected a single, unwavering pair of headlights. He followed all the way to Sector 35, slow, deliberate. Testing me. Measuring me. Waiting for a misstep.

I parked, stepped out, and faced the shadows. He drove past slowly, headlights grazing me briefly before disappearing into the night. Silent acknowledgment. Observation. Understanding. He knew. And he wanted me to know he knew.

Inside my flat, the roses remained wrapped, untouched. My pen tapped against the table, each click echoing the rhythm of my own heartbeat. The city outside was quiet, unaware of what almost happened. I had come within seconds of crossing a line. The hunger roared inside me, sharp and immediate, craving action, craving precision, craving the canvas only I could conceive.

I poured coffee, black, no sugar. The warmth did little to settle the tension in my hands. I traced the patterns across my notebook, reviewing movements, timings, potential vantage points. Each potential tableau mapped in exacting detail, each contingency accounted for. Sebastian's presence lingered in my mind like a ghost, the weight of his observation pressing at the edges of my compulsion.

I imagined the next scene: roses, precise angles, body positioned to speak without words, hands folded just so, eyes wide open, a statement beyond murder; a signature of control, of power, of inevitability. Each petal a punctuation mark, each drop of rain a whisper of narrative.

Yet a small voice; doubt, or fear, or something older; reminded me that he had been close enough to catch me in the act. The thought was almost exhilarating. Almost. The compulsion had not been sated, but now it was sharpened, refined, focused.

I traced the map again, pen hovering. Sector 17, Sector 22, potential exits, potential witnesses, angles of light and shadow. The city's pulse synchronized with mine. I imagined how easily the narrative could be guided, how effortlessly the scapegoat could be manipulated, how the city could remain oblivious while the real story unfolded in silence.

The thrill of proximity, of almost being caught, of knowing someone intelligent, relentless, and observant had been steps behind me, made the compulsion sweeter. The line between observer and participant blurred further. The next move had to be perfect.

Hours passed. I drafted contingencies, alternate plans. The roses would need to remain pristine, the angles perfect, the story undeniable. Each step accounted for, each potential witness considered, each trace managed. The thrill pulsed like electricity through my veins, sharper than the first time I had orchestrated a scene, more acute because the game had changed.

Sebastian's absence in his apartment; his retreat after the silent surveillance; left a tension that pressed against the walls. He was patient, calculated, waiting for the right moment to act. And I knew I was being watched, always, but for the first time, I felt a thrill in that awareness. The presence of another mind close, piecing together the puzzle of me, sharpened my edge.

I leaned back, pen tapping against the edge of the table. The city outside remained oblivious.

Lights flickered, neon reflected in wet streets, distant horns sounded, rain still fell. But the internal storm; the compulsion, the planning, the thrill; roared inside me louder than anything outside.

The canvas waited. The next tableau demanded attention. And Sebastian, patient, precise, relentless, had already begun tracking the threads I had left behind.

I was close to the edge, closer than I had ever been. And the line between observer and creator, between chaos and control, between compulsion and calculation, was thinner than ever.

CHAPTER 21

Bait and Silence

The morning air in the Crime Branch was deceptively calm. Coffee machines hissed in the background, telephones rang with mundane insistence, and the hum of fluorescent lights filled every corner. I stepped inside, folder tucked under my arm, pen tapping against the edge in its familiar rhythm. But the moment I saw Sebastian, seated at his desk with uncharacteristic stillness, I felt the shift. Too calm. Too deliberate.

He didn't look up immediately. He shuffled a few papers, and then, with precision that was almost theatrical, slid a file across the table toward me. "New lead," he said. His voice carried no urgency, no judgment, only a controlled weight.

I raised an eyebrow, letting my fingers drum lightly against the folder. Inside, the photographs made me pause. A warehouse, dimly lit, and at its center, a mannequin posed like the judge's victim: hands folded, head tilted, eyes wide open, red roses strewn across the floor with ceremonial care. A perfect mimicry, yet disturbingly artificial.

I froze for a heartbeat before laughing, the sound brittle, too loud. "What is this? Some rookie's art project?"

Sebastian's eyes didn't flicker, didn't betray amusement or surprise. He leaned back slightly, letting the silence stretch. "An anonymous tip," he said carefully. "Someone out there knows too much about the killer's methods." His gaze met mine, steady and deliberate. "I want to see how you interpret it."

I leaned back in my chair, pen tapping, face casual, voice light. "Copycats breed copycats. Chandigarh loves a spectacle. Maybe this is just a sick admirer playing dress-up."

But beneath the casual mask, my pulse raced. The details were far too precise for coincidence. The tilt of the head, the folded hands, the roses' arrangement; almost exact. Sebastian hadn't stumbled onto them randomly. He had orchestrated the situation. This was a test. A trap.

I tried to shake it off. The Branch buzzed with morning activity, papers shuffled, colleagues moved past in quiet conversations. But I felt the trap pressing in, a narrowing of the space I thought I controlled. Every reflection in the glass walls, every angle of light on the desk seemed amplified.

By afternoon, the tension had not eased. During a team briefing, Sebastian presented a list of "possible patterns" in the murders: dates, locations, professions, the timing of each killing. Everyone scribbled notes. He spoke calmly, logically, guiding the conversation as though no one roomed with him carried any secrets.

I caught my breath when one line jumped out: the roses had always come from the same florist in Sector 17. A detail I had deliberately obscured. My fingers itched to tap the table faster, to destroy the façade of composure, but I restrained them.

"Florist patterns?" I said, letting my voice float with mock incredulity. "Really, Sebastian? Next you'll tell us the killer buys chai from the same stall." A laugh escaped, light and forced, and the room chuckled, tension dissolving. Everyone except him. His eyes held mine, unwavering, calculating. Measuring.

The rest of the briefing moved on, mundane in comparison. But my mind raced, replaying the possibilities: had he always known? Or had he pieced it together from tiny, almost imperceptible hints? The way he lingered, the notes he asked for, the calm in his voice — every calculated motion suggested a man who understood the patterns, perhaps better than I did.

Evening descended with the softness of rain on concrete. I left the Branch later than usual, the city already dimming under the glow of streetlights reflecting in puddles. My flat seemed miles away as I walked down the narrow corridors, the rhythm of my pen echoing in my head like a metronome.

And there he was. Waiting outside my office, the dim light of the hallway pooling over him like a spotlight. He stepped forward, voice soft, deliberate. "Cyra," he said, almost kindly, "sometimes the best way to catch a criminal is to let them believe they're still unseen."

I tilted my head, pen tapping lightly against the doorframe, voice even. "And what if the criminal really is unseen? Just a shadow?"

He didn't smile. His eyes held a weight that almost pressed against me, heavy and deliberate. "Then the shadow is already giving itself away."

Footsteps echoed down the corridor as he walked away, slow, measured, leaving the faintest trace of authority in his wake. The hallway seemed narrower after he passed, the walls closer, the shadows more tangible.

For the first time, I felt the walls of the game closing in. The control I had always exercised over the narrative, over perception, over fear itself, felt slippery. I was accustomed to pulling strings, guiding the city, orchestrating the chaos. But now, someone else was inside the same rhythm I thought belonged only to me.

And the worst part? Part of me wanted to be caught. Not entirely, not consciously, but the thrill, the pull of recognition, the desire for someone to measure me, to see the line I walked between creation and compulsion — it thrilled me in a way I didn't expect.

I returned to my flat, shutting the door, the key turning heavy in my hand. Outside, rain still fell, a muted drumming against the windows. Inside, I unpacked the roses from the bag. They lay untouched. My pen returned to my notebook, tapping in sync with my heartbeat.

I traced lines across the page, connecting sectors, plotting potential scenes, imagining angles of light, the trajectory of footsteps, the placement of petals, the tilt of a head. Every detail mattered. The mannequin photographs haunted me in their still perfection, a reminder that someone else had already started to anticipate me.

The trap he had set was not obvious, not blunt. It was subtle, quiet, like a wire stretched just under the surface, waiting for me to step too far. And I had felt it. I had danced along it, nearly lost balance, and it exhilarated me. The game had sharpened.

Sebastian's presence lingered even in his absence. I imagined him watching, dissecting, calculating my every move, my hesitation, my rhythm. The thought both thrilled and unnerved me. For the first time, I wondered if the predator I had always been could coexist with a mind that understood, anticipated, and waited.

Hours passed. The city outside remained oblivious. Streetlights flickered, puddles reflected fractured neon. Every shadow was a potential witness. Every reflection, a question. My pen tapped without stopping, recording potential routes, vantage points, contingency plans.

I plotted the next scene with care. Roses, angles, light, shadows, bodies placed precisely; not just a murder, but a statement, a challenge, a narrative the city would never understand, except through fear.

And somewhere beneath it all, I felt Sebastian's eyes on me. Patient. Deliberate. Observant. Waiting. He didn't need to speak. He didn't need to act. He simply existed as a presence that changed the rhythm of the game.

Night turned deeper. The city slept, rain turning streets into mirrors, puddles reflecting fractured lights. I imagined myself in the alley behind a bar, the target unaware, the roses ready, gloves snug, hands steady. The compulsion hummed.

And yet, I hesitated. Not out of caution, not out of fear, but because someone else had seen it coming. Someone else had already placed the bait. Someone else was controlling the game alongside me.

I tapped my pen on the table, slow, deliberate. Each tap a heartbeat. Each tap a reminder: the predator and the observer could coexist. For now.

And I knew the next move would define everything. The next tableau, the next signature, the next step. One misstep and the line between creator and prey would blur.

I leaned back in my chair, roses still untouched, pen still tapping. The city outside remained unaware. Sebastian had stepped back, watching quietly. Waiting.

And I understood finally: the game had changed.

I was no longer the only shadow in the rain.

CHAPTER 22

The Second Slip

It was late, the corridors of the Sector 17 police headquarters nearly deserted, the hum of fluorescent lights slicing through the silence. Only the faint echo of footsteps and the occasional creak of the aging floorboards punctuated the emptiness. Sebastian had summoned me to the evidence room, his voice calm and measured when he called. I didn't need to ask why. I already knew.

He stood there with a single cardboard box on the table. Inside lay files, photographs, and a sealed packet marked Sector 11 Judge Case. The fluorescent light above cast shadows across the table, deepening the creases of his face. He gestured toward the box.

"We're re-checking the chain of custody," he said, voice quiet, precise. "You were lead on this, right? Walk me through what you logged."

I sipped from the stale vending machine coffee I carried everywhere, the bitter liquid grounding me. My brain was fogged from long hours, the low buzz of caffeine and exhaustion. Easy. I'd handled dozens of these. Every detail memorized, every line of every report filed, every step mapped in my head a thousand times.

I flipped open the file, pen tapping lightly against the edge of the folder, mind rehearsing the narrative. "Victim found in Sector 11 bungalow, entry point from the rear window, roses scattered in a semi-circle—"

I stopped mid-sentence.

The roses.

That detail had never been written in the original police notes. I had added them later at the scene, with my own hands, my own vision of order. My signature. My art.

I forced myself to continue, masking the hesitation with a cough. "—ah, yes, um, roses scattered as reported by the crime scene unit."

Sebastian's eyes narrowed slightly, his voice low, deliberate. "Funny. I reviewed the original unit notes myself. No roses mentioned."

My fingers tightened around the pen, tapping against the folder to maintain rhythm, to maintain control. "Then maybe the note-taker missed it. You know how sloppy the junior constables are."

He leaned closer, calm, steady, eyes sharp as steel. "Or maybe someone added them later. Someone who wanted the murders to carry a signature."

Silence fell like a curtain. The old ceiling fan hummed overhead, louder than it had any right to be, each blade slicing through the tension between us. My pulse accelerated. Every instinct screamed at me, and yet my hand moved with deceptive calm, pen tapping softly against the folder.

I forced a hollow laugh. "Sebastian, you're chasing ghosts. You've been in this too long. Seeing things that aren't there."

But I could see it in his eyes. He wasn't guessing anymore. He wasn't theorizing. He knew.

The ride back through Sector 22's empty streets was a blur. Neon signs reflected in puddles, jagged streaks of light cutting across rain-slick asphalt. My hands gripped the steering wheel tighter than necessary, the pen I always carried tapping against my thigh, a desperate attempt to cling to some semblance of rhythm.

Sebastian's words replayed endlessly: Someone added them later. Someone who wanted the murders to carry a signature.

Every detail I had ever taken for granted; the roses, the positioning, the angle of limbs; now felt like a trap I had laid for myself. I had always believed control was mine, that perception, fear, and narrative bent to my will. But now I realized that control was an illusion. One flower, one small choice, and the world had shifted under my hands.

I thought of the photos in that cardboard box, of his deliberate calm as he traced the chain of custody, his measured questions piercing the veneer of routine. Every file, every image, every observation now carried weight I hadn't accounted for.

The city outside my windshield was quiet, but I could feel him everywhere: the way his presence lingered in the room, the way his absence now felt heavier than any proximity. He was no longer my partner. He was my hunter.

Hours later, in my flat, I sat at the table, coffee gone cold, pen still tapping. My notes were sprawled across the surface: timelines, locations, victim profiles, patterns. Every connection I had traced, every subtle misdirection I had orchestrated, now seemed fragile. Vulnerable.

I stared at my reflection in the glass window, hollow eyes staring back, lips curled into a smile I didn't recognize. The signature, the roses, the perfection I had always chased; now threatened exposure by the only person who had ever truly seen me.

I went over every movement from the day's review: my hesitation when Sebastian questioned the roses, the cough I forced, the careful rhythm of my tapping. Could he see through all of it? Could he read the rhythm of my mind as easily as he read my notes?

The realization was intoxicating and terrifying. Sebastian had stepped into a role I hadn't anticipated. He didn't accuse. He observed. He waited. He gathered proof, patiently, quietly, like a predator circling prey. And I was prey.

The irony wasn't lost on me. I had built narratives, manipulated perception, orchestrated panic. I had made the city see what I wanted them to see. And yet here I was, caught in the same web I had spun for everyone else.

The night deepened. Rain tapped against the windows, faint and insistent. I imagined the roses lying dormant in my apartment, waiting for my next compulsion, for my next act. The urge hummed beneath my skin, sharp and insistent. But tonight, I couldn't act. Not while he was near, not while he watched, waited, calculated.

Every plan had to be rethought. Every signature, reconsidered. Every step measured against the knowledge that one misstep; even the smallest, most invisible slip; could undo everything.

And I knew now that the game had changed. Sebastian was no longer a supporting actor in my performance. He had become the unseen force altering the narrative, waiting for me to reveal myself fully. Waiting for me to slip again.

I returned to my notebook, tapping the pen slowly, deliberately. My mind traced connections, plotted contingencies. Every potential tableau was now a question of timing, visibility, and risk. The roses, once symbols of my control, were now potential evidence against me.

Sleep was impossible. Caffeine barely touched the fog of adrenaline and apprehension coursing through me. Every shadow in my apartment seemed to flicker with intent. Every sound; the hum of the fridge, the distant siren; carried the weight of Sebastian's observation.

I thought of the other murders, the copycat narrative, Rajiv Malhotra's panic. I had built a perfect world of misdirection, of fear, of control. But Sebastian's words had dismantled it in an instant. One flower. One small, elegant choice, and my world had shifted.

He didn't need to accuse. He didn't need to shout. The knowledge was already present, pressing, undeniable. I had given myself away. And I would have to be smarter. Faster. More precise.

The city slept outside, indifferent to the currents of tension swirling inside my head. But inside me, the hunger pulsed stronger, sharper. The compulsion demanded action. The art demanded completion.

I tapped my pen, tracing invisible lines across the table. The hunter and the hunted were now entwined in a dance neither could fully control.

And I knew it: the next slip could be the last.

The roses, my signature, my canvas; all had betrayed me once.

But I would not betray myself again.

The night stretched endlessly. Rain fell softly, neon glinting across puddles. And somewhere, not far, Sebastian watched, silent, patient, unyielding.

And I, the artist, the orchestrator of fear, had become the prey.

CHAPTER 23

The Silent Tail

Chandigarh nights were deceptive. From above, the city looked orderly, geometrically perfect. Wide boulevards, neatly plotted roundabouts, and the symmetry of streetlights made it appear calm, almost sterile. But the beauty was an illusion. In the gaps; the dim-lit tea stalls, the broken pavements near Sector 22, the alleyways too narrow for a vehicle; shadows lived. Shadows that breathed. Shadows that watched.

I left the station past midnight, leather jacket pulled tight against the sharp September breeze. Coffee in hand, pen between my fingers, I tried to convince myself that Sebastian's suspicion had been nothing more than exhaustion, stress, overworked intuition. Yet the feeling persisted. Something pricked at the base of my neck, a subtle itch that no amount of rationalization could soothe. Eyes were on me. Always.

The Gypsy police jeep I knew too well was parked across the street, engine off, headlights dark. I didn't glance at it directly. Looking would have confirmed the anxiety I already carried. Instead, I walked toward the market line, passing shuttered sweet shops and closed paanwalas, before cutting across to the narrow lane leading to my flat in Sector 15.

My shoes clicked against the uneven pavement. A dog barked in the distance, but I didn't flinch. Then I heard it, the sound of footsteps. Heavy. Measured. Familiar.

Sebastian.

I didn't need to turn. I knew that gait, the subtle shift of weight, the way one foot slightly overreached the other, the tiny cadence that marked a man who had trained his body in discipline. A soldier's walk, a predator's patience. Not aggressive, not frantic; controlled. Calculated. Watching.

So I let the city play for me. I took the longer route past Rose Garden, where iron lamps cast orange halos across empty benches, the fog of the early morning mist curling around them. Paused at a tea cart still open for truckers, pretending to fumble for change while letting my gaze roam. The jeep had pulled up at a distance, dark, silent, patient.

He was tailing me.

But not like a predator stalking prey. Like a father watching his daughter step toward fire; careful, cautious, unwilling to look away, but unwilling to intervene until necessary.

I sipped the scalding tea, letting the burn anchor me. Every detail mattered. Every distraction, every hesitation, could be measured. If he followed too close, I would have to act. If he maintained his distance, perhaps he still doubted, still observed without certainty. Maybe.

I moved deliberately, taking my time through narrow alleys, letting the rhythm of my shoes against the stones mask the pounding of my pulse. Every corner became a calculated decision: pause, glance, move. Nothing left to chance.

When I finally reached my flat, I unlocked the door slowly, deliberately, knowing he was parked just one street away, waiting. I stepped inside, shutting the door behind me with a careful click, the lock securing more than just the threshold. It was my first line of defense, a barrier against the inevitable confrontation lurking in the shadow of the night.

For the first time in years, the silence of my apartment was suffocating. The walls seemed closer, the ticking wall clock louder. Each tick a countdown, each second a measure of Sebastian's patience. The city outside slept, unaware, indifferent. But inside, the tension hung heavy.

Sebastian wasn't my partner anymore.

He was my shadow.

And shadows do not forgive. Shadows do not forget. Shadows wait.

I sank into my chair, coffee cooling at my side, pen tapping against the table. The habit, the rhythm, a thin thread of stability in a room that suddenly felt unmoored. I could hear the faint hum of the refrigerator, the faint buzz of neon from the streets below. But nothing masked the weight of observation pressing in, the knowledge that somewhere, just out of sight, someone was watching.

My reflection in the window caught me; hollow-eyed, tense, lips curved in a smile I didn't fully recognize. The city outside reflected in the glass seemed calm, orderly, serene. But the reality; the truth of the night; was far from it. Someone had seen too much, someone had calculated too carefully. Someone had begun to close the net.

I traced patterns in my mind, paths through the city, past crimes, past tableaux. The roses, the poses, the control I had wielded with ruthless precision. All vulnerable now. One small slip, one overlooked detail, and everything could unravel.

The sound of the jeep engine starting somewhere in the distance made me flinch. He hadn't left. He was still watching. Waiting.

And I knew it with bone-deep certainty: the game had changed. The hunter had stepped out of the shadows.

Tonight, the city slept. But I did not.

I was being watched. And for the first time, I understood that being watched might be even more dangerous than being caught.

The shadows were patient. The city was patient. Sebastian was patient.

And I was running out of time.

CHAPTER 24

Small Intrusions

Paranoia is a small animal. It creeps in on feet no bigger than a whisper, then multiplies until it fills the room and claws at the throat.

After Sebastian began tailing me, nothing stayed the same for long. Small intrusions appeared in the margins of my life, the quiet things that used to go unnoticed. Fingerprints on a glass I knew I had cleaned. A chair ever so slightly moved from its place. The kettle switched on when I was certain I had left it off. The city itself felt too loud with secrets it had never shared before.

The first sign was a note. Cramped, hurried handwriting, left under my door as if it were a thing that hoped to be discovered. *"We watch. Be careful."* No signature. No threat. Just three words that slotted into my chest like a cold pin.

I burned it at first. Crumpled it, cupped it over the gas flame, watched the curls of ash spin and die. But the feeling wouldn't leave. Someone was telling me I was being watched, and someone knew exactly how to make me feel exposed.

Then came the smaller intrusions. My toothbrush moved half an inch to the right in its cup. My coat; the one with the seam that had caught the petal; brushed carefully by a hand that lingered just long enough. Not forceful. Testing. Measuring.

I began checking locks three times. Then five. I changed the passcode on my phone and deleted the last week's call logs like a person trying to unlearn a language. The pen in my hand became an instrument of ritual; *tap, tap, tap;* a prayer against silence.

At the Branch, Sebastian was steady, unflinching. He stopped asking direct questions and began leaving breadcrumbs where I could find them. A photograph of the third scene printed twice; one copy on my desk with a circled detail. An anonymous tip quietly placed in the evidence box, labeled unchecked. He did not need to say the words. Suspicion was in the air between us, sharp and surgical.

I caught him once in the compound, speaking to a junior constable near the florist stall in Sector 17. Steam from my chai fogged my glasses as I watched from the shadowed corner. He asked about delivery receipts, timestamps. The florist shrugged and wiped his hands on his apron. Conversation ended with the clink of change. His face was calm as stone, but his eyes; his eyes were counting.

Night brought worse things. Whispers shaped themselves from the wind along the balcony. My dreams betrayed me. Courtroom benches filled with familiar faces, hands tracing the roses. I woke with pen prints across my palms, as if I had been clutching it in sleep, scratching invisible lines onto the air.

At one in the morning, I discovered my mailbox had been rifled through. Not emptied, just subtly rearranged. Envelopes shifted, a utility bill moved to the front. A message disguised as carelessness. The security guard swore no one had entered after midnight. The stairwell camera showed a thirty-second gap around two a.m. Technical glitch, or someone with the skill to erase the smallest traces.

I wanted to believe it was random. I wanted to blame the city, thieves, bored youths, mundane hazards. But reason felt like a flimsy coat in this weather. Sebastian was knitting the net quietly, stitch by stitch, and I could feel it tighten around me.

At three a.m., I sat at the kitchen table, counting the taps. *Tap. Tap. Tap.* The rhythm steadied me, until it didn't. I stared at the seam of my sleeve where the petal had caught and contemplated confession. A fevered part of me wanted to tell him everything; to strip away the performance and stand bare before the man who had raised me like a parent raises a child. I imagined his face when the truth fell across it; horror, pride, betrayal. The thought thrilled and sickened me in equal measure.

Instead, I planned. Paranoia demanded businesslike action. If someone was watching, I would watch back. If Sebastian tightened the net, I would decide where the pressure built. I would be the hand that cut the rope if it grew too tight.

I slept poorly, but I wrote better. The pen tapped while the city turned. Somewhere in the quiet hum, my pulse learned a new rhythm: suspicion answered by intention.

CHAPTER 25

Maps and Countermeasures

He was patient. I had admired that once. Patience suggests trust. Now it suggested something else: a slow, deliberate measuring of time.

I began setting traps of my own; small, lifeless tests to see if anyone had been in my flat.

I rolled a cigarette and left the pack on the windowsill, unlit. I draped a shawl across the back of a chair and did not touch it for two days. I placed a book half out from the stack on my bedside table. When it shifted a finger-width the next morning, I did not scream. I catalogued.

At the Branch, I began altering minute details in my reports. I wrote a false time in one note and watched to see who repeated it. I slipped a bogus florist invoice into the paper trail, dated three days earlier than any real purchase. If Sebastian was running his quiet audit, the anomaly would draw his attention.

He noticed. Of course he noticed. He is precise; that's why I once trusted him. He lingered over the altered notes, brow furrowed, then checked chain-of-custody logs as if tracing a seam.

One of the junior officers, Rashid, approached cautiously. "Ma'am, Sir asked me to follow up on a call. He wanted to know who you met with on Tuesday night." Casual-sounding, but the leash was in the implication.

"Tell him I met no one," I said, keeping my voice steady. Inside, something churned like an engine. The conversation had become a contest of proximity. He would reach me through others. I would make those others fragile.

I tightened locks again. I moved the roses into a new bag, leaving the old one in plain sight; a decoy. I cleaned my gloves obsessively, then smeared a thin trace of coffee inside one, seeing if anyone would notice. Paranoia becomes scientific.

A pattern emerged. Sebastian moved as if in a ceremony: florist receipts, security footage requests, quiet questions to CFSL technicians, subtle conversations with journalists carrying intentions like hidden messages. He was building something concrete out of suspicion.

And I, who had always choreographed outcomes, found myself for the first time not in control of the dance. It felt obscene.

On a humid Thursday, I saw him again at Rose Garden. Not the stooped, fatherly figure I knew, but a man hunting evidence. The florist handed him a small brown packet, eyes lowered. He followed a path through the garden, packet clutched like contraband. He did not look at me. He did not need to. His patience was methodical; stacks of receipts and time stamps that would make any accusation look inevitable.

I followed from the shadow of a spreading chinar, breath ragged. I had always loved the thrill of being feared. Now I learned what it meant to be hunted.

That night, I emptied my notebooks, burning pages smelling of coffee and confession. I photographed evidence again, leaving copies in old drawers. I scrubbed at the seam where the petal had lodged, pulling threads until the fabric thinned. I tried to remove myself like a stain.

But stains remember.

When I finally collapsed into half-sleep, the city outside was still, neon dimmed to a sleepy smear. The pen lay where I had dropped it, silent. I dreamed of roses; folded, paper, falling from a ceiling no one could see.

Sebastian did not come to my door that night. He didn't need to. His moves were already in motion.

The noose was not only tightening; it was being measured, documented, prepared for a very public snap. I had hours; maybe days; and somewhere in that distance, I had to decide: preempt, vanish, or play the final hand.

I chose to sleep with my clothes on.

CHAPTER 26

The File

Sebastian never raised his voice. That was his style. Anger wastes energy. Patience builds gallows. Every word measured, every pause deliberate, every glance holding more weight than a shouted accusation. I had always admired that about him; once. Now it felt like a weapon trained on me, invisible and inexorable.

I knew he was building a file. The rumors at the Branch were whispers and sideways glances, a current of quiet certainty. CFSL Chandigarh had been asked to re-run specific traces. Evidence from past crime scenes, fingerprints, fiber analysis, even the tiniest fragment of residue on a glove. All of it catalogued, cross-checked, and filed.

A junior constable carried folders from Sector 36, clutching them under his arm like sacred texts. He handed them to Sebastian who didn't try to hide it. He didn't need to. Sebastian's movements were deliberate. Every step in plain sight, and yet I couldn't touch it, couldn't interfere.

I imagined what was inside those folders. Receipts, timestamps, photographs, residue swabs, careful annotations in fine handwriting. Little things I had overlooked; or thought were insignificant; now magnified, connected, and twisted into evidence. Every minor slip, every trace left by habit or compulsion, catalogued. Enough to suggest possibility. Enough to paint intention. Enough to make a magistrate pause before the gavel.

And yet, I had no proof. Only the tightening in my chest, that wherever Sebastian's file existed; his desk drawer, his flat, maybe under lock in the Sector 17 station vault; it was accumulating weight. My name pressed into it like ink on tissue, pressing, staining, undeniable.

I remembered the first time I had felt it; the subtle shift in his demeanor when he spoke my name differently, casually at first, a soft cadence that never used to exist. "Cyra," he said one morning, two syllables, flat and deliberate. No "kid," no warmth, no familiarity. The small change had stung like a scalpel. That was the day I realized the file had already reached the size of betrayal.

I imagined him at his desk late at night, lights dim, pen in hand, filing every scrap of paper, annotating each photograph, tracing each pattern with patience I had never envied until now. Each click of the folder, each shuffle of paper, each underlined note was a step closer to me being caught; not by luck, not by chance, but by the meticulous mind I had once trusted.

My mind raced through contingencies. Could I destroy it? Could I move it? Could I rewrite the past? I traced possibilities in my head like paths across a map, imagining him counting, recording, connecting dots I hadn't even realized I left. And then I stopped. I had nowhere to hide. Not from him. Not anymore.

The strangest part was the thrill, the sick twist of exhilaration buried under panic. I had been so used to being the orchestrator, the unseen hand guiding the narrative, that being observed, tracked, measured, catalogued; it was new. Dangerous. It made my pulse accelerate in ways I hadn't felt since the first time I had staged a body, the first time I had left a trace only I understood.

Sebastian's patience had become an instrument of precision, more terrifying than anger ever could be. He didn't need to yell. He didn't need to accuse. He was building a truth so methodical, so layered, that it could never be ignored.

I touched my pen, tapping against my notebook, trying to ground myself in the rhythm, the only comfort left in a world where I was no longer the hunter. Each tap was a heartbeat, each thought a calculation, each breath measured. I couldn't see the file, but I could feel it, heavy and cold, like snow pressing on a roof, threatening to crush everything beneath.

Sleep became impossible. Coffee, too bitter to enjoy. I moved through the Branch like a shadow, feeling Sebastian's presence at every corner, hearing the quiet shuffle of paper, imagining the slow accumulation of evidence against me. My mind traced the edges of my mistakes, my compulsions, the slips that had seemed insignificant. All of them were now potential proof.

And yet, in that fear, a darker thrill remained. The knowledge that someone saw everything, catalogued everything, made the danger exquisite. Sebastian's file was the noose, but it was also a mirror; reflecting my own obsession back at me.

I lay awake that night, staring at the ceiling, counting the taps of my pen on the desk beside my bed, tracing the imagined lines of the evidence in my mind. Each detail he had found, each anomaly he would follow, was a step closer to confrontation. I knew the file existed. I knew he had it. I knew he would use it.

And the worst part? I knew I couldn't stop him. Not yet.

CHAPTER 27

Paper Cuts

I tested his perimeter. Slipped false invoices into the evidence trail. Delivered contradictory witness statements. The old tricks; the kind that turned investigations into a fog of useless data. Every move was deliberate, every error engineered, meant to mislead, confuse, distract. I had done it countless times. And always, I had controlled the fog.

But Sebastian cut through the fog. He always had.

One evening, I returned to my flat to find a small slit in the envelope on my table. My electricity bill, opened, then resealed. No thief in Chandigarh would care about kilowatt hours. That was Sebastian's paper cut: small, bloodless, deliberate.

When I touched the paper, my fingers shook. For the first time in years, my pen slipped from my hand and clattered to the floor. The tapping that had always steadied me; the rhythm of thought, the heartbeat of control; was gone. Each clack of the pen hitting tile sounded like a gavel. Judgment rendered, verdict delivered.

I circled the flat, eyes scanning corners, corners that had never mattered, doors that had never betrayed secrets. Every object, every shadow, became suspect. My notebooks, once neat archives of observation and deduction, became frantic maps of contingency. Escape routes traced in margins, railway lines out of Chandigarh, bus timetables from ISBT Sector 17, roads that disappeared into the green of Punjab fields. Each plan, meticulous. Each possibility, accounted for.

But running was not my nature. I did not flee. I corrected. I erased. I covered traces I hadn't meant to leave, replotted evidence trails, rewrote timelines in my mind. The city had become a chessboard. Sebastian had become the opponent I could not anticipate, the king I could not corner.

I remembered the first slip; a petal caught in the seam of my sleeve, a tiny fragment I had ignored. Now I understood what that mistake had meant. Every minor lapse, every compulsion, every signature detail I thought secret, was being noted, catalogued, weaponized. He had built a file; no, a dossier; and I had walked blind into it.

I sat at the edge of my bed, pen in hand, not to write, but to steady the shaking. Pages lay open around me, diagrams of routes, timings, footprints, florist receipts, security camera angles, fabricated notes interlaced with actual evidence. The line between my lies and the truth had blurred so completely that even I couldn't distinguish one from the other.

Sebastian was no longer my father figure. He was a liability.

I smoked. The cigarette burned too fast, smoke curling like questions around my fingers. I traced the path of his eyes through the Branch, imagining the meticulous slowness of his investigation, the quiet accumulation of evidence that I couldn't touch. Each question he asked, each photograph he lingered over, was part of a net I could feel closing but could not see.

The thrill pulsed through me; a sharp, cold flame. I had always loved being feared, loved orchestrating outcomes, loved seeing the chaos bend to my design. But this was different. Now the predator moved in silence, and the prey, *me*, was finally visible to someone else.

I imagined his hands moving through the forensic archives, tracing fingerprints, comparing fibers, examining receipts, cataloguing anomalies. Every seemingly mundane interaction was part of the game. The game was no longer mine. It was his.

I thought about my compulsion; the urge, the rhythm, the need to craft scenes, to leave messages in petals and posture, in light and shadow. Now it felt like a chain around my wrist. I wanted to act, to create, to let the canvas speak; but any movement could betray me further. Every rose, every angle, every mark could become evidence in a file I could never control.

I flicked through my notebooks, eyes scanning the chaos of numbers and lines, imagining Sebastian reading them, placing them alongside his observations, building a portrait of me piece by piece. I could almost hear the quiet tick of his mind, the patience of a predator who does not rush, who waits for mistakes.

I knew the worst part: I had hours. Maybe minutes. And somewhere in that distance I had to decide: preempt, vanish, or play the final hand. My thoughts raced like trains in tunnels, each decision branching into consequences I wasn't sure I could survive.

I lit another cigarette. I traced the outline of my hand against the table, the pen resting lightly between my fingers, useless now, silent, the rhythm I relied on broken. I imagined Sebastian opening my drawers, checking my files, comparing timelines, marking anomalies. The precision of his patience was terrifying.

And yet, in the center of it, something inside me stirred. Not fear exactly. Not thrill exactly. Recognition. Respect. Hate. Desire. A mixture that left me dizzy, tremulous, and too alert all at once.

I had once built worlds in my notebooks, orchestrated illusions, bent narratives to my will. But Sebastian had reminded me that even illusions could be traced. And tonight, his trace had been small; a slit in a paper envelope; but it had struck deeper than anything else.

I placed the pen down, finally. My hands shook too violently to hold it steady. I traced the slit in the envelope with a fingertip, imagining the precision of the cut, the patience of the hand that had done it. He had reached into my world without entering it, marking me without leaving a trace.

And I knew this: the game had changed. The noose was tightening, yes, but he was measuring it, documenting it, preparing it for a very public snap.

I had survived every test, orchestrated every chaos, predicted every reaction; but Sebastian had found a weakness I hadn't even noticed in myself.

I chose to sleep with my clothes on.

And somewhere, in the still hum of the city, the pen waited.

CHAPTER 28

The Last Coffee

We sat together one final time, outside Indian Coffee House in Sector 36. The air smelled of damp earth and exhaust fumes, mingling with the bitter tang of roasted coffee beans. The place had been ours for years: sticky tables, greasy cutlets, smoke curling lazily from cheap cigarettes, and conversations measured in sips and pen taps.

Sebastian stirred his coffee slowly, watching the spoon trace lazy circles. His face, carved with lines I had memorized since my twenties, was calm; too calm. There was weight in his silence, a gravity that pulled at the edges of the world. I studied him carefully, tracing the shadow under his eyes, the set of his jaw. A lifetime of small gestures I had once dismissed as habit now felt like threats in slow motion.

I took a sip of my own cup, bitter and hot, letting it burn down to the back of my throat. It anchored me in the moment, a ritual I relied on when my thoughts spiraled. My pen rested on the table beside the coffee, silent. I did not tap. There was no rhythm left to control.

"I suppose," I said finally, voice light, almost teasing, "that this is it. One more case, Sebastian. We'll crack it. Then maybe we both rest."

His eyes searched mine, not with trust, not even with pity, but with certainty. The certainty of someone who knows the shape of your thoughts before you even think them, the certainty of someone who has catalogued your habits, your compulsions, your errors. I almost shivered.

I wanted, for a heartbeat, to confess. To lay down every secret I had carved into petals, postures, and shadows. To collapse into the safety of being known, of being understood. But there was no safety here anymore. Only observation. Only judgment. Only the slow accumulation of proof.

Instead, I smiled, faint, controlled, the smile of someone still playing a game. "You're quieter than usual," I added. "Planning another trick?"

He did not smile. The corners of his mouth remained firm, unyielding. His hand tightened around the cup, knuckles pale, and he sipped carefully, as though savoring each second. "No tricks," he said softly. "Just watching."

The words were simple. The meaning, anything but. He had watched me through years of chaos, through compulsion and obsession, through mistakes I had not realized I'd made. And now, sitting across from him, I understood that I was the one being studied, measured, and; if he chose; exposed.

I traced the rim of my coffee cup with a fingertip, thinking of all the small invasions, the paper cuts, the slips that had led us here. The torn petal, the slit envelope, the notes I had left as bait and countermeasures. All of it had been observed, recorded, folded into a file I could not touch.

I wanted to tell him: I am still in control. I always am. But the words died in my throat. He already knew. He had always known.

Outside, the street moved in oblivion. Neon signs flickered over wet asphalt, the occasional motorcycle rattling past. Life continued, indifferent, while we sat in our private orbit of coffee, observation, and unspoken truths.

I pushed the cup away slightly, letting the bitter dregs settle. The ritual was over. The rhythm was gone. And yet, the quiet thrill of the chase still pulsed faintly in my veins.

I looked up at him one last time. The man who had been my anchor, my mentor, my shadow, was now the one who measured my missteps. The one who knew my secrets. And the one who would decide whether they remained secrets.

"This will be our last coffee," I said softly, and he nodded once. A small acknowledgment, but enough.

We left the table together, footsteps in sync for a moment, then diverging as we disappeared into the night. I carried the taste of bitter coffee and inevitability in my mouth, and for the first time in years, I did not reach for my pen.

Because some stories, once measured, cannot be rewritten.

CHAPTER 29

The Body in Sector 22

Chandigarh woke to another tableau.

A real estate broker, the kind who bullied widows into selling their homes at half price, lay in his Sector 22 bungalow. His throat had been cut with precision, the dark red of the blood spreading across the pale marble floor in a slow, deliberate bloom. Roses were scattered in a spiral around him, each petal placed with a meticulousness that suggested more than cruelty. It suggested ritual.

The stench of iron and death mingled with the faint smell of disinfectant from the cleaners who had tried to touch the scene before the crime branch arrived. I inhaled it in, letting the sharp tang fill my senses. Death had texture; it had a smell that pressed itself into your lungs and whispered. And yet, I didn't feel horror. I felt recognition. I recognized the geometry, the signature.

The media had erupted by the time I arrived. Headlines screamed, "Copycat Strikes Again!" Their panic thrilled me. Rajiv was already in custody, yet here was another victim, a perfect mimic, as if the city demanded spectacle. It was absurd, delicious, intoxicating. The officers fumbled, torn between defending Rajiv's innocence and acknowledging the impossibility of the scene. I moved among them with practiced calm, pen in hand, notebook open, as if I were merely documenting the work of another, not my own creation.

"This," I said, crouching near the victim, voice low and measured, "isn't Rajiv's work. He was locked in a cell when this man died. We're dealing with a second killer. Smarter. Closer."

They nodded. Their trust in me was automatic. They didn't know I had orchestrated the first bodies. They didn't know the thrill I'd felt placing petals, positioning hands, choosing angles. They would never suspect that I was standing over a scene that could have been mine in an alternate hour, my own compulsion nearly satisfied.

Not Sebastian.

He didn't speak. He didn't need to. He stood in the corner, coat collar high, hands deep in pockets, eyes locked on me with a patient intensity that made my spine tighten. It was worse than accusation. Worse than fear. It was certainty. He saw what others couldn't, even before the file in his drawer could articulate it.

I let my gaze drift over the scene again, deliberately slow, cataloguing every detail for them, for him, for me. The spiral of roses, petals clinging to the slick marble where the blood had pooled, some smeared across the hands as if the man had tried to touch them in his last seconds. The head tilted at the perfect angle, eyes wide, staring; not at death, but through it, to some empty sky only I could see.

I imagined myself in that pose. Hands folded, roses pressed against my chest, eyes staring wide into nothingness. The thought made my chest tighten. The thrill and terror coiled together, sharp and electric.

I traced the trajectory of the spiral with my finger, careful not to touch the blood, memorizing the rhythm. Each petal, each inch of marble, was a heartbeat, a punctuation, a statement. I wondered if the officers saw it, if they felt it, if they could sense the compulsion that had drawn the previous scenes into being. They did not. Only I understood.

Later, back at the Branch, the tension remained unbroken. I spread out my notes, moving my pen across the page in neat, obsessive arcs, as if mapping the unseen lines between the victims. Sebastian slid a photograph across the desk. One partial bootprint in the corner of the scene. Familiar. Too familiar.

"Funny," he said quietly, "how the pattern matches your shoes."

I forced a laugh, hollow and brittle. "You're reaching, old man. Half the city wears Bata boots."

He didn't reply. He didn't need to. His eyes held the knowledge that my mind was already trying to repress; the creeping truth that I had left a mark, a clue only he could recognize.

My thoughts spiraled. What if the next tableau didn't satisfy me? What if someone else had started to mimic me? Would I be caught, exposed as the artist of a city's nightmares? I could almost feel the hunger returning; the craving for control, for composition, for the ritual of creation. My hands shook lightly, craving paper and pen, craving roses, craving the cold smoothness of marble under fingertips.

Sebastian's patience gnawed at me. Every quiet move he made was a blade, measured, deliberate, precise. He didn't yell. He didn't accuse. He catalogued. He documented. And I; who had always been the unseen conductor of death and fear; was suddenly visible.

I imagined the next body: the arrangement, the lighting, the petals floating in perfect alignment with blood still wet. My pulse raced. The city was a canvas, my compulsion a brush. But I also imagined Sebastian there, hovering in the corner of the room, eyes steady and unblinking, file open, proof accumulating.

I felt the thrill of creation and the terror of exposure coil inside me, inseparable. And I understood fully that the hunt had changed. I was no longer the predator. I was being measured, mapped, and pursued.

And worse? I wanted him to see it all. I wanted him to watch me unravel, to catch the edges of my madness before they spread fully. The compulsion surged, a craving I could not resist, a hunger with a rhythm I had no control over.

The net was closing. And I was dancing inside it.

CHAPTER 30

The Spiral

The city has a rhythm. Wide streets, measured roundabouts, traffic lights blinking red, amber, green like a heartbeat that refuses to rest. Chandigarh never changes its pattern. But I had.

Since Sector 22, the rhythm inside me had fractured. My pulse refused to sync with the city's. It skipped, tripped, faltered, like a record scratched in the middle of a waltz. I could hear

Sebastian's silence in every corner; in the pause before a constable answered a question, in the Commissioner's eyes lingering too long on me, in the empty chair at the canteen where he used to sit, calm, paternal, observing.

He wasn't calm anymore. He was waiting. Patiently. Calculating. Watching.

I began cataloguing exits the way normal people catalogue friends. ISBT Sector 17. Chandigarh railway station. The highway through Zirakpur toward Ambala. Each route ended in the same word in my notebook: escape. But escape didn't fit me. I wasn't a fugitive. I was an artist. Artists don't abandon their work halfway. They see it to its final stroke, even when the canvas screams beneath their hands.

Sebastian's file had weight now. I could feel it pressing against the air, even when it wasn't in front of me. Somewhere in that manila folder were the roses, the boots, the gaps in my notes, the slip of a tongue when I recalled what I shouldn't have. A case strong enough to pin me down in a courtroom, lights glaring, witnesses staring. Unless the file was destroyed. Unless the hand holding it was erased.

I thought about him often in those nights. The slight tremble in his hand when lighting a cigarette. The way he still, sometimes, called me "kid" when the mask slipped. The careful, deliberate cadence of his steps through the Branch, the low hum of his voice when speaking to subordinates, the way he believed in justice, in order, in rules written on brittle paper. He had raised me inside that system. He had been the only father I had ever allowed myself to claim. And now… he was the last obstacle between me and survival.

I traced my pen across the table, three beats, pause, two beats, over and over, until it sounded like a countdown. I imagined it all; a walk through the Rose Garden after rain, the gravel slick and glinting under the dim street lamps. His footsteps echoing before mine, heavy, certain. I would meet him, calm, steady, affectionate, words laced with trust and memory. And the knife would slide from my sleeve. A final correction, clean, efficient.

I pictured the bloom of roses at our feet, petals slick with rain and dirt, blood hidden beneath the layers, the city's geometry unaware of what it had witnessed. I told myself it wasn't murder. Not really. It was an ending written into the story from the beginning, a father and daughter meeting at the edge of a lie, a narrative snapped neatly at the spine.

I stared into my reflection in the window. The fractured city lights shattered across the glass, making my face look like a puzzle with missing pieces. Hollow eyes. Lips curled in a smile I did not recognize. Hands poised, fingers itching for motion, for creation, for erasure. The reflection whispered to me, mirrored my obsession, amplified my hunger.

I traced the spiral in my mind; the body, the petals, the knives, the file. Each step had a rhythm. Each heartbeat a command. The world narrowed to a single point: Sebastian. And when he fell, the last tether to the version of me that could feel guilt, fear, or love would vanish with him.

I whispered to myself: He will not take me down. He will not end my story. I will.

The pen tapped faster now, erratic, jagged, mirroring the pulse in my chest. I drew lines on the notebook, maps intersecting with timelines, pathways and contingencies. I imagined every possible intervention; witnesses, cameras, patrols; and folded them into the plan like origami. Nothing would touch me. Not him, not the law, not the city that had once been my canvas.

The thought was intoxicating. The thrill of control, of finality, coursed through me. Every corner of my mind whispered the same word: perfection. Every act, every motion, every breath was a step toward it.

And in that whisper, the plan solidified.

Sebastian would die.

And when he did, so would the last version of me that had ever been human.

Because survival demanded art. And art demanded blood.

CHAPTER 31

The End of the Net

The rain had turned the pathways to mud, but Rose Garden still smelled of life. The petals gleamed wet, heavy, bowing under the weight of the storm. Streetlamps flickered, their light fractured by dripping branches.

I walked slowly. My boots sank into the gravel, crunch muted by water. My hand curled around the knife's handle in my coat pocket, slick with my own sweat, fingers trembling with anticipation.

He was there, waiting.

Sebastian.

His figure leaned against the stone bench near the central fountain. Even through the haze, I saw the rain-darkened coat clinging to his frame, hair plastered to his forehead. In his hand: a file. A swollen manila folder, edges curling from damp.

My file.

"You came," he said. His voice cut through the rain, steady, calm. Like he knew I would.

I forced a smile. "You called. I listen."

His eyes were old tonight. Not tired, not broken; just old. He placed the folder gently on the bench. "Do you know what's inside?"

I tilted my head. "You tell me."

"Pieces of you," he said, tapping the folder. "The roses. The timings. The things you remembered too well, the things you shouldn't have known. It's all here. Took me weeks to admit it. Months, maybe. But once you see it…" His throat tightened. "…Cyra, you've been writing your own confession."

The rain drummed harder. My heartbeat hammered louder.

I stepped closer. My fingers tightened on the knife. "So what now, Sebastian? You drag me to Sector 17? Book me under Section 302? Make me the villain in your story?"

"No," he said softly. "I came here so you could tell me the truth. Not as your superior. Not even as a cop. As…" His jaw clenched. "…as the man who raised you."

The words cut sharper than the steel in my hand.

My throat burned. "You think I didn't love you?"

"I think," he whispered, voice breaking for the first time, "you're lost. And I didn't see it soon enough."

The silence between us was a grave. The rain fell like shovelfuls of dirt covering it.

I pulled the knife free. The metal caught the flickering light, a spark in the downpour. His eyes flicked to it, then back to mine. He didn't flinch.

"Cyra," he said, low. "Don't."

But I could feel the inevitability burning inside me. Rage at being known, at being seen through, at the love I never wanted to admit I needed. One step closer. Two.

I lunged. The knife bit into his coat, slipping past the fabric, scraping against the muscle beneath. He didn't dodge. He didn't flinch. The knife found the first line; a shallow cut along the shoulder, a crimson bloom blooming against his raincoat.

He gasped, wet and surprised, but his hands stayed by his side, steady. His eyes didn't leave mine.

I thrust again. Harder. The knife sank into him; through fabric, into flesh. His mouth opened in a silent scream I didn't hear over the rain, his eyes widening.

Another blow. Then another. My movements were a mix of rage and ritual, precise, frenzied. Each strike punctuated by the rain, each tear of flesh a punctuation mark in the sentence I was writing across his body.

He stumbled, leaning against the bench. Blood slicked the marble beneath him. I didn't stop. Not until the file slipped from his hands, soaked, pages splayed across the wet stone, water and blood merging like ink.

His coat was shredded, his chest a lattice of red lines. He sank to his knees, coughing, hands clawing at my boots, mud and petals smeared into a grotesque mosaic.

"I… Cyra…" His voice faltered. "Kid… it's… not too late…"

I shook my head. One final slash, clean, precise. The knife bit into his neck. Blood sprayed in a staccato against my coat, my boots, the wet petals beneath us. His eyes widened, glassy, and then the light in them died.

The rain washed over us, turning the garden into a canvas of red, petals and mud and blood mingling into a spiral of chaos. His body toppled forward, spilling across the fountain steps. My breathing was ragged, hands trembling, knife dripping, reflection fractured in the puddles around me.

I dropped the knife. It sank into the mud with a wet thunk.

Sirens wailed in the distance. Flashlights cut jagged lines through the storm. I didn't move. I didn't run. I only stared at him, at what I had done.

The city was silent but for the rain. The roses glistened, heavy and red.

And somewhere deep inside, a part of me; long buried beneath rhythm, patterns, and compulsion; whispered: Art is never incomplete.

I walked through the rain, boots wet with blood and mud, leaving the last man who had ever loved me behind.

And the city waited, oblivious, for its next rhythm to resume.

TO BE CONTINUED ...?

About the Author

Oh, Banapsha, the daydreamer who thought spinning stories was just a chill time until reality hit her with a job title. Then she got slapped with a massive dose of imposter syndrome, and her book dreams did a total faceplant into the pit of self-doubt. Epic fail, right?

But guess what? Instead of cranking out novels, she started pouring her heart out in a creative diary – like, therapy for her wild imagination that sometimes tripped into straight-up fantasy land.

And oh, the plot twist! As her messy musings got real, a legit story emerged like a boss phoenix rising from the ashes of her wannabe-author dreams. Suddenly, those scribbled rants turned into a full-blown series. Who'd have thought her coping mechanism, originally just to keep her own chaos in check, would become a rad escape for others?

Passion for writing, you ask? We'll see if she's just flexing, or is the real deal.

https://www.authorbanapsha.com/

Connect with Banapsha! *(She can be a pain in the behind, but you know, she's cool n'all) ;)*

Acknowledgments

I am profoundly grateful to my mother, *Praveen Kumari*, and my maternal family, whose unwavering support has been the bedrock of my journey. Though they may not know anything about the book (Or that they are mentioned in the acknowledgments of it), but their presence has been my constant. Thank you for your unconditional love and belief in me.

A heartfelt thank you goes to *Veer Malhotra*, my proofreader (and a *huge* pain in my behind). Your expertise and dedication elevated this work beyond my expectations. Even though I *hated* you when you were pointing out mistakes, I do realize how important that was. (I did not like being told I was wrong.) Your insights and keen eye has left an indelible mark on these pages (literally), and for that, I am *truly* grateful.

Mayank, your design prowess breathed life into our author website, adding a visual dimension to the words. (Yes, the website was made by this guy. He did ONE good thing in our friendship, but who's counting.)

Last but certainly not least, I extend my deepest gratitude to the readers who have ventured into the world I've crafted. Your time and attention are invaluable, and the fact that this work has found a place in your hands is both humbling and heartening. This book is close to my heart, and it means the world to me that you are here with me. I genuinely am so, *SO* grateful to each and every single one of you. And I hope you all a *lot* of good *everything.* Scratch that. I wish you all the *best* of *everything.* Once again, thank you so much for being here.

Thank you, from the bottom of my heart to everyone mentioned above (and anyone I missed), for being a part of this literary adventure.

With sincere appreciation,
Banapsha

Thanks for reading!
If you wish, do share your reviews with me!
I am keenly waiting to read all your thoughts!